# THE
# *Refiner's Fire*

*Also by Lee Kingman*

*Break a Leg,* Betsy Maybe!
Escape from the Evil Prophecy
Georgina and the Dragon
Head Over Wheels
The Peter Pan Bag
The Year of the Raccoon

# THE
# *Refiner's Fire*

## LEE KINGMAN

HOUGHTON MIFFLIN COMPANY
BOSTON 1981

Printed in the United States of America

V 10 9 8 7 6 5 4 3 2 1

*Library of Congress Cataloging in Publication Data*
Kingman, Lee.
    The refiner's fire.

    Summary: Thirteen-year-old Sara goes to live with a
father she hardly knows in a New Hampshire barn which
they share with a community of artists.
    [1. Fathers and daughters—Fiction.   2. Communal
living—Fiction.   3. Artists—Fiction.   4. New Hampshire
—Fiction]   I. Title.
PZ7.K595Re        [Fic]         81-6313
ISBN 0-395-31606-5             AACR2

To all the potters and the painters
and the singers who enrich my life,
especially R.H.N.

# 1

"He's done it again," Sara decided. "He made a promise, and I've come all this way, and he isn't here to meet me. He's abandoned me."

Across the street from the drugstore that served as bus stop for the small New Hampshire town was a white church with a steeple that seemed to be admonishing an indifferent sky. Near the base of the steeple was a clock with bold black numbers and hands. It had stated the time as five minutes past one when the bus stopped to let Sara off and she discovered no one was there to meet her. That didn't surprise her, even though it bothered her. Her father had never been a clockwork person. He'd always skipped along on his own time.

Now the clock insisted that it was five minutes of two. "That isn't just being late," Sara worried. "He forgot I was coming."

She looked up and down the quiet street as another thought needled her. Perhaps he'd been inside one of the stores, looking out the window, and he hadn't recognized her now she was taller and thinner and he thought she hadn't come, so he'd gone away.

Perhaps she wouldn't recognize him! The last time she'd

seen him, more than four years ago when she was not quite nine, she'd had to look up at him, up past the wavy strands of his reddish beard and his drooping mustache, to catch the glint of his eyes behind his wire-rimmed glasses. Those eyes, his whole manner, had always seemed expectant, waiting for something from her, and she'd never been sure of what that was — of what would please him.

She stood there now, alternating between the fear that her father had abandoned her and another fear — that when he did appear he would still expect far more from her than she was prepared to give. Yet this time she would have to meet his expectations. She had no other choice. She would have to overcome the clumsiness that had frustrated so many of her childhood attempts to get along with him.

A pickup truck rushed along the middle of the street, veered, and rammed to a stop at the curb by her clump of baggage. A clean-shaven man, only a few inches taller than Sara, slid from the truck and strode purposefully toward her. His hair was thinning and fuzzed up from his forehead. His nose was slightly crooked and his mouth a bit thin-lipped. He was not wearing glasses. He was smiling and he bounded up to her, his hands outstretched.

"Sara? Saradipity?" he asked — and then she was sure. Only her father had ever called her Saradipity.

"It's me. Are you really Richard?" That was another of his eccentricities, never wanting to be called Father or Papa or Daddy. "Such nonsense," Gran had said. "Fathers are meant to be fathers. He acts as if your mother went out and ordered you one day from the bakery." Gran had never approved of Richard Bradford, the strange man her daughter had married. He had been a roving scholar who had dragged his wife and child all over the world while he studied the history and art of ceramics. "He may call them pots," Gran complained, "but pots to me are pans. What he writes about surely look to me like plain old dishes."

"I am indeed Richard," the man said, quite formally for a father speaking to a daughter. "The current version, that is. No longer the scholar of pots — the D.D. — the Doctor of Dishes. I am now the potter himself. Which is why I am a little late. I had to pack an order to send in the afternoon mail and I just made it. I hope you didn't mind the delay?"

He expected an answer. What could she say? Sara shrugged. "It gave me a chance to see what there is to see in Martin's Corners," she said tactfully.

"Let's load up." Her father looked at her baggage. "What is that?" He pointed to the small traveling case with grillwork set into it. "Did you bring a pygmy woolly mammoth along with everything else?"

Sara eyed her father. He was, she suspected, being amusing. Or thought he was being amusing. It was hard to recall, after so many years away from him, exactly how his sense of humor worked. She did remember that he liked people who considered his remarks witty, so she laughed. "How did you guess it's a pygmy woolly mammoth?" Until she was sure of how he felt about her, she'd take her cues from him.

Actually she hoped she'd handed his idea back to him neatly enough for him to dismiss it, and she hoped she didn't have a guilty look. She knew her father did not like cats. Inside the case was her cat, Fonzie.

"Well, what's done's done," as Gran would have said. Sara had a choice: take Fonzie to the animal shelter for whatever fate that held, or bring him along with the rest of her worldly goods — the "everything else" her father had mentioned — which consisted of two suitcases mended with tape and a large paper sack with string handles that held things she couldn't fit into the cases. Among them was the ugly china cat Gran had rolled into newspaper and stuffed into the bag. Something about that cat bothered her. She wished now she'd left it in Yellow Creek, Tennessee.

Her father bent over the case. "How do I pick this up? Gingerly? Will it snarl?"

"It might. You'd better let me do it." Sara picked the case up carefully, hoping Fonzie was so groggy from his two days of traveling with her on interstate buses that he was asleep. She reached over the tailgate and set the case down.

"Ready to see your new abode? Your new dwelling place?" Richard asked. He liked asking rhetorical questions and using less-common words. Like abode and dwelling place for house.

"Of course I want to see it." How could he ask, when he'd kept her waiting so long? Then she remembered his remark about having to reach the post office in time to send out a package. Could there be a changed attitude along with those changed looks? "Do you like making pots instead of studying them?" she asked.

"I do!" he said with enthusiasm. "All that scholarly detail began to seem dusty. So I thought, why not shape the forms myself? Why not become of the earth earthy and perform the craft I studied so long?"

"Is it fun?"

"It is fun I take very seriously."

That was her father, all right. Full of contradictions. He

had confused her when she was little, and it looked as if he was going to go on confusing her. That much hadn't changed. Sara sat beside him in the truck, determined to make the best of it: to survive whatever lay ahead, just as she had somehow survived her childhood spent in strange cities among strange people whose talk she couldn't understand. Her mother had not survived. She had died of dysentery in the north of India when Sara was eight. Richard had attempted to cope with his daughter on his own. Even by his unfatherly standards, the venture had not been a success; so he had brought Sara to her mother's mother in Tennessee.

Her years with Gran had been a haven of ordinariness. Sara had had a room under the eaves where she felt secure; Gran had put her hot breakfast on the table every morning and her wholesome supper on the table every night; she had made and kept friends; she had planned contentedly to stay in Yellow Creek right through high school.

Then it became clear that Gran couldn't keep house anymore because she had developed severe emphysema, and the least little bother left her, she said, as breathless and useless as a busted balloon. She had to have oxygen and injections to pull her back into shape. Sara could do the housework quite well, even though she had just turned thirteen. But not the nursing. Reluctantly, Gran had written to Richard in care of his lawyer, and a week later, Richard had phoned. The conversation was brief. Send Sara to him in New Hampshire. He was settled down at last. Sara could live permanently with him. Gran wasn't to worry.

"He's claimed before he was settled down," Gran had said, "and it never took. Let's hope for your sake he means it, because I'll have to sell this house. There won't be any place for you to come back to, this time."

"I know. I'll have to get along with Richard no matter what he does. Or where he goes."

"Men like Richard Bradford don't change," Gran had announced. "All twinkle and sparkle and charm on the outside. He draws people to him the same way those little plants down by the swamp draw flies — those sundews that glitter and shimmer and entice poor bugs right into their trap. Then they feed on them."

Sara knew her grandmother was a keen observer of character, but hoped Gran's pronouncement wasn't true. She didn't want to leave the security of Gran's arms and eaves and discover her father was no better than a glittering, carnivorous sundew.

"Stand up to him," Gran had warned her. "Don't let him twinkle you to death. Like he did your poor mother."

"I'll try," Sara promised.

For the moment, as Sara and her father drove along, she couldn't think of anything to say to him. He loved to sing, and he was humming a few phrases over and over, with his mind apparently more on the music than on Sara. She looked at the passing scenery: small hills and rocky pastures, tracts of scrubby growth, worn-out farms, and stands of pines struggling up from sandy soil. They passed a few well-kept houses and yards, but most of the places were small, some little more than shacks or old trailer homes, with huge woodpiles in the yard, some with abandoned cars and broken-down trucks and tractors.

"Around here it used to be small farm country," her father told her. "Scrabble farming on poor soil, but one family would

6

live and work in a place for generations. White farmhouses and red barns all around. Beautiful barns! In fact, that's where we live — in a barn."

"A barn!"

"I have the most noble barn you've ever seen. It's one of the largest in New England, so I needed help from other people to fix it up, and by the time we finished making it useful, several of them wanted to stay on, to work there, and live there. They help with the pottery and they have their own crafts, too. It's turned into a communal effort. You'll love it."

Sara looked doubtfully at her father. The idea of living in a barn struck her as full of difficulties and discomforts compared to Gran's house, and the idea of sharing it with others was a surprise. Yet Gran was right. Her father did seem to operate on a sundew principle, drawing people in to share his life.

"So it's like a commune," Sara said.

"I don't care for the word *commune* — not to describe us, anyway. There should be a more artistic word for a group of craftspeople. You know the odd words they give to groups? Like a gaggle of geese or a pod of whales or a mob of kangaroos? It should be a help of workers or a display of craftsmen or a wheel of potters."

"Or a brush of painters?" Sara ventured. She liked word games.

"Good for you! You always were bright, Saradipity. You couldn't get out of your own way sometimes. But bright."

So her father hadn't forgotten Sara's pattern — all the things that, despite her eagerness to do right, came out wrong. She changed the subject. "Is there a house that goes with this barn?"

7

"It burned down years ago."

"So you live in the barn?" She was anxious about rooms and bathrooms and being alone in a cozy place if she needed to be. "How can you cook and wash and be warm and — "

"And clean and tidy and elegant?" Richard continued. "My dear little princess Sara, where is your sense of adventure?"

Sara could sense that her father was disappointed in her, and she squirmed as he went on. "After I tried to bring you up adaptable to castles or hovels, riches or rags, Cordon Bleu cuisine or raw fish! I have failed in what I now understand is called *parenting*. It used to be known as Being the Old Man." He put the back of his hand to his forehead in a mock theatrical gesture, and Sara giggled nervously.

The laughter pleased him. He enjoyed an audience and Sara certainly could be that. "Tell me about who lives at the barn."

"First, there's Zeke Gardiner, who lives up to his name because he does our gardening. He helped fix up the barn and he's stayed on as our general handyman. He's also a deer-hunter, a stew-cook, and he knows all about wood. He finds seasoned wood for the partitions in the barn and hardwood for fuel in the stoves and slab wood for firing the kiln. He likes to whittle, and with a little encouragement from me, he's started to carve animals and designs. He's really good. Sometimes he helps in the pottery."

Sara thought Zeke sounded interesting, especially since he could cook. She was already suspicious about what her father expected her to contribute to his communal effort. Cooking? Cleaning? She hadn't minded housework for Gran, who encouraged her with praise rather than giving critiques of her

8

efforts. But housekeeping for a barnful of people? "Who else is there?"

"Ben Tillsit. He's six feet six, weighs almost three hundred pounds, and has huge hands that take to wood tools with the skill of a surgeon. He makes superb furniture. His hair and his beard are carroty-red. He came driving in one day, looking for work space in a barn. So he joined up, swapping space for carpentry. And there's Gabe Courbeau. He'll be a good companion for you. At least he's nearer your age. He's fourteen."

"How did he come to the barn?"

"I bought some goats from the Courbeaus, who live down the road. The goats kept running back to Gabe. Then he'd have to walk them back to me. We talked about a lot of things, and after his old man beat him up worse than usual, Gabe asked if he could live at the barn and look after the goats and help in the garden. So we made him resident goatherd and he helps in the pottery as well."

"That's three men besides you! Aren't there any women?" There'd better be! Sara thought.

"There's Blanche Wicketts. Blanche is beautiful."

"Oh?" Sara was impressed by the admiration in her father's voice. "How old is she?"

"Are you wondering if your old man has fallen in love? Let me tell you!"

Sara sat still, barely breathing. Deep in an inner chamber of her romantic heart, even deeper in a sequestered niche of her conventional brain, was a wish: that since she had to live with her father again, he would marry and once more provide Sara with a mother. Sometimes in a lonely moment, a memory would overwhelm her and make her lonelier still. Yet it was

9

more a sensation than a memory, as if she could still smell a faintly flowery aroma that drifted up from her mother's hair and still feel the warmth of her cheek and softness of her breast. Sara had an ache to be held and comforted and loved by a mother, and perky bony little Gran, who found it hard to demonstrate affection, had never cured the ache — a hug from Gran was like a pinch from a nutcracker. "What about Blanche?" Sara asked.

"Blanche has the most gorgeous eyes I've ever seen. And an ample figure. Hugging Blanche is like squeezing store-bought bread. She sighs and flows back into place all over herself."

That sounded promising, Sara thought.

"Her hair is like silk and it's purest white." Richard gave Sara a mischievous smirk, as if he'd read her hopes and teased them along until he could deliver the punch line. "Blanche is already married, and she's over seventy years old."

"Oh!" So Blanche couldn't solve the mother-problem. Sara hoped for the next best thing. "Does she cook and do the housekeeping?"

"She takes her turn, but Blanche considers herself a crafts-person. She crochets things in dreadful Day-Glo colors." Richard gave an exaggerated shudder. "Maybe they're tams for bald babies. Or skirts for flowerpots. Anyway, they're little ghastlies. It's her husband, Harvey, who's the craftsman. He makes miniature furniture to scale. His work is so exquisite that I can forgive Blanche her crocheted excrescences."

"How did they come to live at the barn?"

"They were gypsying around the country, going to craft fairs in an old trailer, and when I met them at a fair last spring their trailer had just died and was too expensive to fix. They were tired of traveling, and when I offered them a spot in the barn, they moved right in."

"They sound nice. I could use a grandmother-type. To make up for Gran."

"Do you miss your grandmother already!"

"Of course. She was all my family for four years! All I had from you was postcards." Sara couldn't help letting her voice turn edgy, even though she knew it would be irritating. She could hear Gran saying, "Don't let him twinkle you."

"You need not rub that in, Sara." Richard spoke calmly but firmly. "I am aware of my deficiencies as a father. But things have changed. I shall be so fatherly that you won't even remember all that. Now — also at the barn," he went on, "is a young woman named Kyra. She has a little boy, Demetri. I had better explain, before you meet her, that Kyra isn't just living at the barn. She is living with me at the barn. You know what I mean when I say 'living with'?"

Sara did. Gran hadn't provided any information about sex, but Sara's girl friends had. "You mean sleeping with?"

"Exactly," said Richard.

Sara's hope for an instant mother rose again. "Then why don't you marry her?"

"Kyra's a fine painter. She's independent, and she doesn't want to marry me."

"Oh." From the tone of Richard's voice Sara gathered that the situation was complicated. Yet at least it was a possibility. She intended to work on it. Even having an instant brother might not be too bad. Sara began to look forward to the barn and its inhabitants, and with each rise up over a small hill or a new curve in the road, she watched for the first view of her new home.

# 2

"There it is. Isn't it awesome?" Richard Bradford braked the truck as it nosed over a crest in the road. Sara stared across a valley at the imposing structure rising up from a hillside.

It was indeed a barn. Not the sensible kind of painted, two-storied, hay-lofted barn attached by a woodshed to a comfortable New England farmhouse. This was a weathered-wood, unpainted giant of a barn determined to mark the landscape with its presence. Even the rows of windows flashing in the brilliant sunshine seemed to be sending signals. There was not another building in sight, and its immensity, as well as its isolation, did awe Sara. It made her uneasy.

I'll be trying to sleep in there tonight, she thought, and staring up at — what? Huge beams shrouded in cobwebs? Barn owls swooping out of the rafters and dropping mice on me? An ache of homesickness for her haven at Gran's caught her up. She managed to stifle a groan into a cough.

Richard took her strangled grunt to mean he'd knocked the wind out of her with his elbow as he shifted gears to ease down the hill. "Sorry! Hang in there. All my life I've wanted to own a home, and at last I do!"

There was her father being confusing again — calling a

12

barn a home. Yet she had to reward his delighted smile with a smile of her own, even if it merely skimmed the surface of her face as briefly as a stone skipping over water. She remembered living in some very strange places when she was little and how cold and uncomfortable most of them had been. This could be as bad. The hope and eagerness she'd experienced only a few moments before vanished.

Richard drove up a dirt ramp and stopped in front of the barn, where the sliding doors were open. The inside was so vast and dim that Sara couldn't see through to the far end. Richard jumped down eagerly from the truck and let out a yodel. To Sara's surprise an attempt at a yodel came back, accompanied by the flat rattle of cowbells. Above them from an open window came the sound of a stereo playing symphonic music. Somewhere below, in the depths of the barn, a powersaw screeched. The entrance to the barn, reached by the ramp, was on its third level, and there were two floors above and two floors below.

"Might as well drive right in. Then we won't have to carry things so far." Richard got back into the truck and drove it into the barn. Sara stepped down onto a rough-timbered floor that was oil-stained from years of housing tractors and farm machinery. Piles of objects whose uses she could only guess at rose up like rubble-strewn pyramids. She saw old water tanks and tractor tires, rolls of cattle fencing and barbed wire, blocks and tackles, tangles of rope, piles of lumber. How did her father expect her to feel at home in such dirty confusion?

Richard noticed her dismay. "Cheer up, Sara. This is still the *barn* part of the barn. Up those stairs, on the next floor, are the common rooms, and up on the top floor there is a bedroom just for you. Come on. Bring your pygmy woolly mammoth or whatever it is. By the way, I hope it is *not* a cat."

Sara didn't look at him, and she didn't say anything. Perhaps she could keep Fonzie in her room, and in such a huge place, her father would never know the cat was there.

He carried her suitcases, and she took the sack but left the cat cage to move when her father wasn't around. At the top of the stairs was a large area that served as a living room. There were three couches and some upholstered chairs excavated from secondhand shops. Green plants hung by the uncurtained windows, and there were several sturdy tables and benches. In one corner was a pool table and in another, a Ping-Pong table. "Whose are those?" Sara asked, as they seemed totally out of character for her father.

"They came with the barn. Left by a guy who went broke trying to fix this up as a ski lodge. It's too far away from the mountains."

Beyond was a large kitchen where a picture window allowed anyone working at the sink to gaze out at fields and woods. Even on such a warm day a black wood stove was in use, with a teakettle and a stewpot seething away on it. There were mugs and plates set out on a big table by another picture window. Open shelves were well stocked with staples in glass jars, and a collection of cooking utensils hung on the wall near the stove.

"Someone's in for afternoon tea," said Richard.

"It's me, waiting for you." A dark-haired young woman stepped out of an alcove by the largest refrigerator Sara had ever seen. She put a dish of butter on the table. "I'm Kyra. Welcome to the group."

Kyra didn't reach out to Sara, even to shake hands. She was

going to let Sara take her time and make her own moves, yet Sara felt the friendliness in her voice and her smile. "Sara would probably like to see her room, Rich, and find the bathroom. Then come back and we'll have a snack."

Now she'd had a longer look, Sarah realized that Kyra was quite a bit younger than her father. Her short curls were damp, and her olive skin gleamed from the afternoon heat. Her nose was a bit bony, but you didn't notice it much because her brown eyes were so lively. No one could have been more different in looks from Sara's mother, who had had long red-gold hair she wore up in a twist and eyes that changed from blue to green.

"I am starving," Richard announced. "I must have missed lunch. How about you, Sara?"

"I had breakfast way back in Connecticut."

"Let's get you settled quickly then." Richard took her up to the top floor, which seemed something like a hotel. A corridor down the middle led past lots of doors, some open, some closed. "There are two bathrooms on this floor — and here's your room."

He led her into a corner room now awash in sunshine. One window looked down on the ramp and the other out to the hill rising up beyond the barn. The furniture consisted of an army cot with a sleeping bag, a table, a webbed lawn chair, and a white-painted bureau. The walls were finished in white sheetrock. A single bulb in a Japanese paper lantern hung on a cord over the cot.

"It's not fancy, but you can fix it up any way you want, and we'll hunt up a better bed soon. See you in the kitchen." He whistled on his way along the hall.

Sara looked out at the spacious view over the hillside. Gran's house had been enclosed by trees, surrounded by other houses. Inside there had been a hushed dimness, in which she and Gran had moved in daily patterns, as serenely as fish in a bowl contented with their contained, half-lighted world. Here everything was so unshaded, so brilliantly lit, that she was dazzled by the openness. She was, suddenly, a fish out of water — gasping at the penetrating air.

It was confusing, too, to find that her father was different — and yet the same. Even in his absence he'd provided her with both nightmares and daydreams. Which was it going to be this time: nightmare or daydream? Or both?

Her stomach grumbled with hunger, and she hurried to the kitchen. Richard sat at the table, making himself a sandwich and trying to describe to Kyra a green color he had noticed on a poplar tree. "It's a mellow color. Not a rugged color."

"How can I tell a color from words like that? Name a rugged color."

"Easy," said Richard. "Scarlet. Turquoise. Orange. All the shrill colors. Wait till you see the autumn leaves here. You'll paint like a maniac."

"I only do that on Crete. I'm doing so badly here I should go back there."

"What do you mean — go back to Crete!" Richard was startled. "You have terrific possibilities with all that's around here. With this landscape. With the changes of the seasons. With me. With all of us here in the barn."

"The world according to Richard! You know I'm a warm-climate person. Ice and snow don't appeal to me."

A little boy skipped in and ran to Richard. They enjoyed a lavish mutual hug. When he settled onto her father's lap, Sara noticed his huge black eyes and how tough and brown his body was. Energy crackled out of him.

"Demetri, this is my daughter Sara. Tell her hello."

"Hello." Demetri looked Sara over carefully, but he didn't say any more. Sara was curious about Kyra and Demetri, who lived on Crete but spoke good English. Was Kyra an international traveler like her father? Did she paint at a place for a while and then move on to another warm-climate country?

A blond young man came in. He smiled at Sara. "Hi. I see Richard found you at the bus stop. I'm Zeke. Rich, do you want those bags of powdered clay in the truck off-loaded into the pottery or the storeroom?"

"The pottery. Would you mind stowing them? I'll come down when I finish eating."

That reminded Sara of Fonzie, who was probably as thirsty and hungry as she was. She'd better rescue him before Zeke or Richard found him in the truck. "I forgot something. I'll be right back." She hurried down the stairs. As she came near the truck she heard Fonzie protesting from his box.

A huge, red-headed man had heard the cat too and stood by the truck. He greeted her with a smile. "Hello. You must be Sara. I'm Ben. Is that your cat carrying on like that?"

"Yes. He's hungry and thirsty!"

"I hope he's a ferocious barn cat who'll be a good ratter."

"Are there rats in the barn?" Sara felt a shiver of goose bumps. She'd anticipated owls and mice and spiders, but not rats. She had never seen a rat, but she was sure they were not as amusing and mannerly as they were made out to be in books.

"Don't be scared. They won't sneak up to the top floor and

17

nibble your toes. They live in the bottom of the barn — the next floor down, where my shop is, and below that where the pottery is. Let's see your cat."

"His name is Fonzie." Sara opened the case and the cat rose up, snarling and stretching. Ben cupped a hand over the cat's back, stroking him gently. "He's handsome. Of course I'm partial to folks with red hair. Now we'll see if he's partial to me."

He placed the cat on his shoulder, and the bright orange color of his hair and of Fonzie's fur were remarkably close. The cat stopped yowling, kneaded Ben's denim shirt with his paws, and then snuggled along his shoulder, rubbing his head against Ben's neck. Sara was relieved that her cat had made a friend, especially since her father didn't like cats. Yet she felt somewhat betrayed as the cat made up to Ben. She wasn't sure she wanted to share him.

It had been strange, too, that she'd felt displaced when she saw Demetri so at home in her father's arms, for she didn't even have any special memories of sitting contentedly in her father's lap.

"Here." Ben plucked the cat from his shoulder and handed him to Sara. "Bring him down to my shop any time, and we'll see if he knows what cats should do."

Sara put him back in the case and carried him upstairs. She wanted to sneak a dish and some milk up to her room to feed him, but when she found Demetri was the only one still in the kitchen, she set out Fonzie's food there. Demetri had taken off his shorts and sandals and sat naked in the soapstone sink, dripping water over himself with a sponge. He held a bottle of dishwashing detergent up and squeezed it and watched the green liquid drop like gems in the sunlight. He hummed as he spread it over himself. Then he dripped more water out of the sponge and, as he splashed, a fleet of translucent bubbles flew up from his body. Then he rested his chin on the sink rim and watched the cat.

"He's a tiger?" asked Demetri.

Sara started to say, "No, silly, he's my cat." But she caught the pretending glint in the little boy's eyes. "He's a royal tiger. His name is King Fonzie."

"He will live here? In this palace?"

"Do you call this a palace?" Sara's sense of pretend was out of practice. She was having enough trouble pretending the barn was a home.

"It's a palace." Demetri stood up in the sink, his body glistening with suds. "I am the prince. See my jewels!" He slapped his chest and more gleaming bubbles flew up. "I am a magic prince. I can ride lions and tigers. I can fly!"

Suddenly Demetri jumped out of the sink at Sara. She tried to catch him, but he was so slippery that he slid through her hands and landed on his knees near the cat. He reached for Fonzie, yelling, "Tiger! Tiger! Ride a tiger!"

Fonzie spit at him and streaked out of the room with Demetri screeching after him and Sara rushing behind them. The cat headed down the stairs and toward the open barn door. The truck had been moved and no one was there to catch the cat. Out Fonzie ran.

When Sara reached the doorway there wasn't a glimmer of orange fur anywhere. Not in the bushes below the ramp. Not down in the trampled dirt yard that ran beside the bottom level of the barn, where she could see Ben, Zeke, and Richard unloading bags of clay from the truck.

To the right of the ramp the ground level was the same as

the middle floor of the barn. Sara saw Demetri standing by one of the raised garden beds, eating lettuce. He was totally content without his clothes and apparently used to plucking fresh snacks from the garden. He pulled up a radish, shook the dirt from it, and polished it by rubbing it on his chest.

He waved the radish at Sara. "Want one?"

"No thanks. Where did Fonzie go?"

Demetri shrugged. "Maybe the tiger hides in the jungle."

"Where's the jungle?"

Demetri pointed up the hillside. Near the top was a tangle of trees and scrubby bushes. Again Sara heard the tinny rattle of bells, and now she saw there were goats tethered in the shade of the trees. But she didn't see Fonzie.

Demetri held out his hand. "Come around the palace."

She followed Demetri through the garden. Aside from the lettuce and the radishes, she didn't have any idea what the plants were. A grassy slope angled steeply past the back of the barn. A deck had been built out over it, one end almost touching the ground and the other having a ladderlike stair reaching down to the dirt yard at the lowest level. A cherry tree, which grew on the hillside a few paces above the barn, shaded the deck, and a rope with a large knot at its end dangled from one of its branches.

A lithe figure stood up in a crotch of the tree and suddenly gave a yell. "Ya–ta–hullew–hullew–oop!" It was less than a Tarzan's signature but more raucous than a yodel. A boy reached for the rope and launched himself, swinging over to thud down on the deck. He let the rope whiz back, and it missed Sara by inches.

"Hey! Watch it!" She scowled at the boy. He wore a T-shirt and cut-off jeans. His arms looked as if he did a lot of

Tarzaning around the trees and the barn. His dark hair was wavy, not quite shoulder length, and he wore a sweatband like a tennis player's. He had the kind of tan that comes from working outdoors, and his eyes were almost as large and black as Demetri's.

"Are you Sara? I'm Gabe. Hi."

"Hi. You could hurt somebody, letting the rope go like that!"

"No way. You ducked. Want to try it? It's a great way to cool off."

"I'm not that hot, thanks." Sara was annoyed because she thought the boy had been showing off to catch her attention. He had caught it all right — more than she wanted to let on. She was even more annoyed when she had to crab-scrabble down the slope while he swung gracefully down the ladder from the deck and then stood there, staring at her awkward descent.

Until a few months ago, Sara and her two best friends in Yellow Creek had talked about boys more than they talked to them. Then Bethy-Sue discovered it didn't seem to matter so much what you said to a boy as how you said it. Soon she and Laura-Ellen were spending more time talking to boys on the phone than they were to Sara. Sara, however, either hadn't gotten the knack of it yet or else she'd talked to boys who couldn't communicate any easier than she could, so they gave up after a few strangled sentences.

Sara wondered what Gabe thought of her after his long stare. At least he seemed curious about her and he wasn't at all shy.

"Richard says you're going to help in the pottery. Are you as good at throwing pots as he is?"

Sara was startled. Remembering her butterfingered past, she wondered why her father would think she'd be useful in a pottery. "What's the idea? Does he expect everyone to make things? I've never made a pot in my life."

"Then probably he wants to teach you. Just like he's taught me."

"Sara!" Richard caught sight of her and looked pleased that she was exploring. He ushered her into the pottery and Gabe followed. "You see around you the efforts of Bradford Earthforms. Not the most inventive of trade names, but sensible. It says who we are and what we do. On the shelves you'll see the pots we've been making for the last three weeks. They're greenware. That means they haven't been bisque-fired yet, so they'll break if you touch them. You have to wait for pots to be bone dry before you fire them or they'll explode." He pointed out the rows of large bowls that lined the shelves. Sara thought it was odd to call them greenware, as the clay was more gray or brown than green.

"There's my biggest order yet," Richard said with pride. Sara saw a bowl resting on a table. She wondered if she could put her arms around its rim, it was so huge. It was deep too, and it rose from its base with a graceful curve. Near it lay a ladle with an arched handle and rows of delicate punch cups. "It's a special order to be used at a wedding reception and then presented to the bride and groom. There's one hundred cups there, as alike as we could throw them, right, Gabe?"

"Right!" Gabe was pleased that Richard made a point of his having helped with the cups. "Have you decided how you're going to glaze them?"

"I want them to glow like sun shining through mist. That means using a lusterlike glaze. I'm testing it right now." He pointed to a small test kiln on a table. "This is a well-equipped shop, Sara — we have three potter's wheels and two electric kilns, and did you notice the wood-fired kiln in the yard?"

"That thing that looks like a brick igloo with a chimney?" Sara had wondered what that was.

"That was the first thing we built after we made the barn livable. You can get fantastic glazes in a wood-fired kiln because of the smoke. Of course, sometimes what happens is glorious and sometimes you have a disaster. Opening up a wood burner after a firing is as nerve-racking as an opening night on Broadway. But it keeps you amazed at the possibilities."

As Sara looked out a window toward the kiln, she saw a flash of orange.

It was Fonzie. A hound, his ears streamlined by the chase, barked after him. They were headed right for the shop door.

Gabe yelled, "Mickey! Stop!"

Sara called, "Fonzie!," and ran to catch him. She wasn't quick enough. The cat's momentum had the force of a missile. He shot through the door and, leaping high onto the table, rocketed right on into the punch bowl. His claws dug into its thin clay walls. With breath-stopped horror, Sara saw the clay crack. Huge pieces fell onto the ladle and the cups, breaking many of them.

She rushed to grab Fonzie and stumbled against the table. More cups fell over and broke. Fonzie leaped again, landing on top of an electric kiln, where he arched his back, flaunted his tail, and hissed.

Demetri screamed, "My tiger! My tiger!"

Richard was enraged, and like the ogre she remembered from her nightmares, he clenched his fist, raised it above his head, and shook it violently. "I'd like to stuff that cat into the kiln and pull the switch."

It was a frightful scene — the most disastrous beginning to her new life with her father that she could have imagined. She was sure Richard meant every word he said. Sara stood motionless, frozen into place as if someone playing Statues had called, "Still pond! No more moving!"

# 3

"Remove that cat!" Richard Bradford bellowed. "Take him out of here and keep him out of here."

Sara was still unable to move or speak.

"What's the trouble?" Ben's form filled the doorway. "Havin' a crashin' good time in here?"

"No. Wreaking havoc, that's what we're doing in here. An uninvited cat, which I assume belongs to Sara, has demolished a two-hundred-dollar order due to be delivered in three weeks."

"Couldn't you throw another punch bowl like that one?" Zeke asked. "And make another ladle? Gabe and I can make more cups."

"It's a matter of time. Not for the throwing. For getting the greenware dry enough to bisque-fire and then have time to do the glazing and refiring."

Sarah knew she should reach up for Fonzie and take him away, but her father stood between her and the kiln, and he still wore a fierce look.

Ben dropped a hand gently on her arm, reached around Richard, and removed Fonzie to a perch on his shoulder. As before, the cat nestled close. Kyra, hearing the hullabaloo, came running too. She picked up Demetri. "Calm down. There's no need to yell."

"I'm sorry, Richard," Sara said in a voice she thought was loud, yet came out as a pained whisper. "I'm so sorry. It's all my fault."

"Don't be stupid, Sara. If Gabe's dog hadn't chased your cat, it wouldn't have happened. Of course, if you hadn't brought the cat in the first place — " Her father unclenched his fist and lowered his arm, and then, seeing everyone staring at him, he tried to lighten the tension. "It's nobody's fault. Dogs chase cats. Cats leap into unfired punch bowls. Potters get up tight and scream. Don't look so unstrung, Sara. I knew you didn't have a pygmy woolly mammoth with you. I knew it was a damn cat and I'd have to make the best of it. Tomorrow we'll start making another set, and if the gods are with us and bless the final glaze firing, we'll make the wedding reception."

He took a dustpan and brush off the wall and began to clean up. Gabe swept the floor. Kyra led Demetri out of the way.

"Now you've seen Richard's shop, how about coming to see mine?" Ben invited Sara, giving her a chance to retreat.

Accepting it gratefully, Sara said, "I'd love to."

Ben kept Fonzie on his shoulder as he led the way. His shop on the next floor had as much bewildering machinery as the pottery. Along the unwindowed back wall were all kinds of tools that matched their silhouettes painted on a pegboard. A heavy carpenter's bench held vises and planers and sanders. The front of the room contained piles of lumber stacked to dry.

Ben placed Fonzie on the floor. The cat took a few steps and sat down, puzzled by the sawdust that clung to his paws. He tried licking it off.

"Hey!" said Sara. "Is sawdust good for cats to eat?"

"It's full of fiber and cellulose. I hear they even sneak some into food for humans now."

When Fonzie curled up in a chair, Ben said, "Fonzie's a sensible cat. He'll find places to stay out of Richard's way. And Mickey's."

"Does Mickey belong to Gabe?"

"Yes. He's usually friendly and lazy. If Fonzie leaves him alone, I doubt there'll be any more chases. They just surprised each other."

"And my father!" Sara sighed and turned a spindle she'd picked up around and around. Ben found a little job to do quietly. Sara sighed again and burst out, "Why did it have to happen! I couldn't have got off to a worse start with Richard. Just when everything has to go right."

"Has to?" Ben asked. "You got a life-or-death situation here?" He leaned against a bench, giving her time to talk if she wanted to — and to her surprise, she did. Ben looked so calm, so massively ready to solve anything.

"When Richard couldn't keep me with him before, he took me to Yellow Creek to live with Gran. This time I can't go back to her. She's too sick. I wanted everything to go smoothly with Richard, so he wouldn't mind having me around the

26

way he did when I was little, and I always seemed to be in his way."

A lonely, empty feeling surged over her and tears filled her eyes. "Damn it," she said, as the tears overflowed and spilled onto the bench, pocking little craters in the powdery sawdust.

Ben asked, "When did your father meet you in Martin's Corners? About two hours ago?"

"That's right. Not even two hours — but one big disaster."

"And you're afraid that's ruined everything?"

Sara nodded.

"I doubt that very much. Sure he can act like a tempest. I've seen him be as furious as he was now and heard him say things he didn't mean when he calmed down. You didn't really think he would put your cat in the kiln and pull the switch, did you?"

"Well — almost." Maybe not in the daylight, thought Sara. But in my nightmares —

"Then don't give up so soon. I never met anyone like Richard Bradford before." Ben was silent a moment, ordering his thoughts. "He's easy to know on the surface. He's enthusiastic and open and full of exciting ideas he hopes to lay on others. I wouldn't be here if he hadn't made me feel that a group of craftsmen living and working in a barn could be a great experience. He can get along with an old fellow like Harvey Wicketts and a kid like Demetri. He's a warm person."

"I noticed." Sara thought of Demetri fitting himself so confidently into Richard's arms, yet she didn't remember his ever opening up to her like that. "You see, I was never any good at pleasing him when I was little. I even heard him say once that I didn't like to be hugged, and that wasn't true. I did —

but he hugged too hard. He didn't know how strong he was, and when I cried and Mother told him why, he stopped hugging me. I thought he didn't like me anymore."

Ben was surprised. "When you're little, things aren't always the way they seem to you. Maybe he didn't know how to take care of a little girl in those faraway places he's told us about. Maybe he was afraid he wouldn't be a good father."

"Maybe." Sara did feel guilty, talking about her father that way, especially to someone she'd just met. Yet Ben had given her a new point of view to consider. She picked up Fonzie. "Thanks for letting me see your shop."

"Stop in any time," Ben invited.

Sara found her way to the top floor of the barn. Fonzie wriggled restlessly, so she let him go. It amused her to see him stop at an open door and peer in, just as she was tempted to do. He strolled into the room.

"Oh you are a beautiful kitty! Where did you come from?"

Sara followed him. A large woman sat on a tatty chaise longue, sorting balls of yarn. "He's mine. I hope you don't mind cats."

"Not at all. So you're Sara! I'm Blanche Wicketts. Forgive me if I don't get up, but if I move I'll discombobulate everything."

"Yes, I'm Sara and the cat is Fonzie. I'm going to try to keep him up here because he broke a big order in the pottery."

"Oh my! Was your father there?"

"Yes. He yelled at Fonzie."

"Poor kitty! Richard does carry on sometimes. I hope he didn't swear at you. He could shout 'Fribble!' or 'Gobbledyhoicks!' and get as much venom out of his system." The woman sensed that Sara was suffering more than the cat.

"Maybe he shouted, but tomorrow he'll be sitting at that wheel, singing at the top of his voice and throwing another whatever-it-was to take its place."

"It was a punch bowl. A giant one. And a ladle. And cups."

Blanche looked over her half-glasses at Sara. "I'll tell you something. I heard Richard say if he had time he'd change the shape of that bowl. And the ladle too. Now he'll have to make new ones, and he'll be happier because he did." ·

"Why didn't he tell me that?"

"He probably will, in his own good time. Do you play cribbage? I need to take my mind off not having an afternoon snack. I'm dieting and I'm terribly cross when I'm hungry."

"Gran taught me when I had chicken pox."

"Bless your Gran!" Blanche wriggled onto her feet and little balls of yarn that had been engulfed in the folds of her lap cascaded onto the floor. Fonzie and Sara both pounced on them.

Blanche handed Sara a basket. "Drop them in here. I'll find the board and the cards."

The yarn half-filled the basket. Sara set it by the chaise, and Fonzie immediately stepped into it, kneaded himself a nest, lay down, and closed his eyes. "Do you mind my cat in your yarn?"

"No. I wish I could make yarn out of his fur. That color's marvelous." She pulled a coffee table next to the chaise, and Sara dragged up a hassock. "I play cut-throat cribbage, so look out!"

They cut for the deal, and Blanche snicked the cards out with precision. Sara hadn't played for a while, so Blanche declared, "Two practice hands and then it's for real."

Whenever Sara took time to look about her, she was comforted by the Wicketts' room. There were patchwork curtains at the windows, structures of bright-colored string and yarn as wall decorations, along with some exquisitely framed but poorly painted watercolors. There were big braided rugs and a double bed, with a curlicued brass headboard and footboard, covered with a spread crocheted in many colors.

"It's your crib, dear. Aren't you going to count it?" Mrs. Wicketts was smiling at her. "I wouldn't want to double-skunk you in our first game."

Sara blinked at the cards in her crib hand. There weren't any points in it. Mrs. Wicketts double-skunked her.

"Well," said Blanche, noting Sara's frustration, "you're a smart player, but you didn't have the cards. I'll challenge you to a fifty-game tournament. Loser treats winner to a hot fudge sundae with nuts and marshmallows at the Martin's Corners drugstore. You have to win to save me from what my doctor told me was 'fatting myself to death' and I should win so I can keep my good disposition and you don't spoil your complexion."

Sara laughed. She liked Blanche. She wondered if she would like her husband, Harvey, too.

"Thanks for the game, dear. Now I should give Kyra a hand in the kitchen. How cooking does put temptation in my path! Leave the kitty in the basket. He'll move on when he's ready."

Sara went along to see if she could help. Kyra said, "Gabe's gone to bring the goats in. Would you ask him to milk them right away and bring me the milk?"

Beyond the barn Sara discovered a path leading through tall grass mingled with daisies and buttercups. She picked a few as she strolled. She sensed Gabe was there under the trees

30

at the top of the hill. He was pretending not to watch her, just as she was pretending not to know he was there.

She saw four goats — a kid running free and three adults on tethers. The kid bounced over to his mother, who eyed Sara and stamped her foot. Sara had always thought of goats in terms of small, brown kids in flowering Alpine meadows playing sweetly with Heidi. The Nubian nanny facing her now was large. Her shiny black head looked hard and bony. Her long ears curved out like sugar scoops and her eyes, staring with such a strange slanted slit of yellow pupil against the black iris, seemed curious indeed, as if the being inside were peeping out between dark curtains. Sara held out the daisies and buttercups for the kid to munch. He lipped them over thoughtfully.

"Hey!" Gabe came at her in a rush and grabbed the flowers. "Buttercups are poisonous — to humans anyway. So I doubt if they're good for goats either. I've never seen them eat any."

"Sorry! I didn't know." Sara was surprised at Gabe's intensity. He was more concerned for the goats than for her feelings. Yet she was grateful that it was Gabe who caught her mistake — not her father. "Kyra sent me to tell you she needs the milk."

"Okay. Do you like goats?"

"I don't know. I never met any before."

"So — I'll introduce them. The little one is Kiddie. His nanny is Bella. The other nanny is Stella, and the billy is Fella. Quick to say. Easy to remember." Gabe unhooked the tethers. Bella shook the bell at her neck and lowered her head at Sara.

"Will she butt?"

"She's too lazy. Go on, Bella." He gave her a shove toward

the path. Bella stepped off and the others followed. Sara wandered along too, interested in seeing Gabe milk the goats.

He took them through a door under the deck into the bottom of the barn, where their stalls were some distance from the pottery. He plucked a three-legged stool out of a corner and sat down to milk. "Keep Kiddie out of the way, will you? He thinks all Bella's milk is his."

Kiddie was wiry, bouncy. He had ridiculous long, spiky eyelashes and glanced out from under them like a flirt. Sara put her hand out to pat him, and he jumped aside, looking surprised, as if he suddenly found himself on stilts when he meant to be dignified.

"Why isn't a baby goat as cuddly as a lamb?" Sara asked. Not that she'd ever cuddled a lamb, but she expected one would feel as soft and huggable as its fleece looked.

"Goats are smarter. They're independent. Sheep are dumb."

"How do you know?"

"My father has sheep. They're dirty and stupid and stubborn. Goats aren't stubborn. They have character."

Sara leaned against the wall and listened to the psst-plink of the milking. Over in the pottery Richard was singing. Some of Sara's happy memories were of her father's singing. He had a fine voice, and when they had lived in Italy, where opera seemed to cascade out of every other open window, he had taken lessons. She remembered he had liked to sing grand passages from operas and oratorios because, he had told her, "they are full of sound and *furioso*" — an odd phrase that had lodged in her mind.

What he sang now sounded as if it came from an oratorio she'd heard on the radio at Christmas.

"*Thus saith the Lord* — " Richard's voice stepped the notes down, dark and full. *"The Lord of Hosts. Yet once, a little while, and I will shake —* " He shook the notes out and then rolled them back up the scale. " *— the heavens and the earth, the sea and the dry land; and I will shake —* "

The words seemed inappropriate down there in the depths of the barn, where even the strongest voice, proclaiming it would shake the heavens, the earth, the sea, and the dry land, couldn't tremble a timber.

*"But who may abide the day of His coming? Who shall stand when He appeareth?"* Richard sang on with a passion and richness that made Sara's spine tingle.

*"For He is like a refiner's fire."* The tempo quickened. The notes built up into the flowing patterns of the *roulades* — the frilly tricky vocal bits that Richard managed easily in full voice and velvet tones. The phrase *like a re–fi–i–i–i–i–i–ner's fire* came again and again, elaborated upon and embellished. The barn walls acted like an echo chamber. Sara found herself awed and exalted by the sound. No wonder Richard loved singing such a majestic piece of music.

Gabe was impressed. "How come he's not a professional singer? He could be with a voice like that."

Sara wondered too. "I guess he could have been — if he'd wanted to — except we never stayed in one place long enough. My Gran said Richard never liked to be tied down to places or people or things. So he'd enjoy singing lessons for a while for fun. Or being in a concert for a performance or two. But he wouldn't like to do it year after year. It's like his being a potter now. He got tired of studying and writing about pots, so now he's making them. In a year or two, he'll probably want to do something else."

Gabe stared at her. "After building that wood-burning kiln

and spending so much money fixing up the pottery and the barn? And getting this group of people together?" Sara could tell he was surprised that anyone would put so much energy into a project unless it were a lifelong commitment.

"Maybe I'm wrong. Maybe my father really has settled down at last. I hope so."

"I should think so!" Gabe picked up the milk pails to carry upstairs.

Sara shrugged and followed him, suspecting what Gabe thought wouldn't make any more difference to Richard than what she thought.

The phrase *the re–fin–er's* fire kept curling its notes around in her mind. She wondered what it meant. At the supper table she asked, and Richard explained eagerly. He loved to explain. "A refiner is someone who purifies something. His fire burns away the impure parts of it. Say, like getting a certain metal out of an ore that has a lot of other elements in it. Intense heat, or fire, is one way of doing that. It's an ancient way because the phrase goes back to the Bible and probably before that."

"When you fire pots in a kiln, are you refining them?"

"No. When you fire pottery, you're fusing it, so it gets tough and hard, and you're also fusing the glaze onto the clay. By the way, Sara, don't worry about that crash." Richard spoke casually. "I had time this afternoon to throw another punch bowl. Actually the shape is better. So I should thank you for the accident."

Sara stared at her father. How could he have acted at the time as if the demolition of the punch bowl set was a major catastrophe and now as if it hardly mattered! Did he have

34

any idea of how his rage had frightened her? If he did, he must expect her to forget as quickly as he did.

"I guess you'd better thank Fonzie," she said, and then had the pleasure of seeing her father look surprised at her speaking up to him. That gave Sara a whole notch of confidence.

# 4

Sara opened her eyes slowly, because she knew someone was watching her and her feet and legs were numb. She was used to the comforting weight of Fonzie on her feet as she slept, but this felt much heavier.

What she saw were the dirty bottoms of two small bare feet, and beyond that, Demetri's bright red shorts, his brown shoulders, his black hair, his intense eyes staring at her. The upper part of his body lay across her legs, and Fonzie, also on her legs, curled into Demetri's arms. He wiggled his toes at her.

"You sleep hard." Demetri stroked Fonzie, who purred.

"Oooof! Get off my feet, will you?"

"Are you getting up?"

"Ummm." Inside the sleeping bag, Sara felt as torpid as she would have on a summer morning in Yellow Creek.

Suddenly Demetri sat up, and the cot unbalanced and turned over, dumping them onto the floor. Fonzie yowled. Demetri laughed, and Sara, stuck in the sleeping bag, hit her head and bit her lip. She untangled her arms, pulled the bag zipper down, and tried to wiggle her way out. Her feet zinged with pins and needles. She wondered how long Demetri had parked himself on her.

He lay on the floor enjoying his fit of giggles. Sara didn't think anything was funny. She pried her nightgown away from her sticky body. It was wrinkled, as if she'd spun like a top in it.

Demetri said, "I sleep in my nothing."

"I would too, if I knew someone wouldn't be staring at me when I got up. Now get out, so I can dress."

"Why? Can't I see your nothing?"

"No. You can't."

"Why not? I see Kyra's nothing. And Richard's nothing."

"Because I don't want you to. Go on — " Impatiently, Sara pushed him away. He hit out at her, dug in his toes, and took off like a sprinter. She slammed the door. She didn't want to be awakened and find the privacy of her sleep invaded. She was shy about herself and her body. Nothing in her life with plain and modest Gran had prepared her for a small boy who sometimes wore clothes and sometimes did not, or for his casual remark about his mother and her father, with or without their clothes. She realized uneasily that her wish that her father might marry again hadn't taken all the aspects of togetherness into consideration; it might be more difficult than she'd thought to fit into her father's life.

She'd been too tired to unpack the night before, and one suitcase lay open on the floor. She poked around in it for clean underwear and a shirt and shorts and then decided to put her things away. She only had a few dresses. She folded most of her clothes — sweaters, shirts, skirts, shorts, and slacks — into the bureau drawers. The other suitcase held shoes, her favorite books, the little dolls collected by her mother in each country they lived in or wandered through, and Sara's own large rag doll, whose original printed features had to be imagined by anyone who didn't know her and love her as Sara did. Her name was Esmerelda, and while Sara had not spoken out loud to her for several years, she often addressed her silently, for she still felt the doll absorbed her complaints and gave back a large measure of comfort. Sometimes more than Fonzie did.

Sara righted the cot and sat Esmerelda on it. Then she put her books and her doll collection in the set of shelves under the window. She had moved in, and that was that. Except for the paper sack. She knew her rubber boots were at the bottom of it and her yellow slicker was there too. And her yellow rain hat. She might as well have traveled by ark as by bus, she had been so well prepared for rain. And there was the bundle wrapped in newspaper that Gran had thrust in at the last minute, saying "Watch out for this. It's breakable. It was in the trunk with your mother's clothes. It might be valuable, and you ought to have something from your mother to keep."

"What is it?" Sara had asked.

"A china cat. It's not very pretty, but you like cats. Anyway, take it along."

Sara picked up the bundle and pulled off its mummylike layers of paper. Then she almost dropped it, for the memory of what she didn't like about it came flashing back to her, and it made her wince and shiver. The cat stood about a foot high;

its ceramic anatomy was inaccurate, and its unrealistic face shone with a cold white glaze. Its puffy cheeks and its bulging black eyes made it look as if its gilt collar was choking it. Its head was turned to the left. The cat had been one of a pair, the other having its head turned to the right. For some reason her father had treasured them, and each time the Bradfords had moved, her mother had packed them, rolling them up with her soft clothing.

Sara was the one who had broken the right-facing cat of the pair. She had been quite little, but she remembered that they were living in rooms crammed with furniture and ceramic bric-a-brac. The cats were on a mantelpiece above a small fireplace. Sara had thought Esmerelda would look better on the mantelpiece than the cats, and she had climbed up on the fender to put the doll there and, in doing so, knocked over one of the cats. It had smashed onto the marble hearth into pieces too fine to glue together. Her father had heard the crash and suddenly stood before her, his arm raised into a fist as he yelled at her. The lamps in the parlor behind him threw his shape into silhouette. He was a huge black giant about to strike her, a figure who became the ogre of her nightmares.

Yet Sara couldn't remember now whether he had struck her or not. The memory seemed to be revealed to her in sequences, like the shifts of scene in a film. For a moment her mind-camera focused again on the shattered white china on the dark marble hearth. Then it cut to her father in the pottery yesterday, shaking his fist and pronouncing what he would like to do to Fonzie — and then back once more to the china cat that seemed so smugly to sum up Sara's relationship with her father: a fragile relationship that could be as diffident as the cat's semi-smile, as frustrating as an inanimate object's lack of response, and all shatterable — and irreparable — in a second. Her first impulse was to drop the cat out the window, let it break into its inevitable pieces — and forget it. But in some odd way it presented a challenge. Its very smarminess made Sara want to outsmart it — to prove that the cat didn't have any meaning after all. She'd fit into life in the barn, and soon her father would accept her for what she was — his daughter who didn't always get things right the first time, but was willing to try.

Blanche's door was open. She sat on her chaise, crocheting, and called, "Great morning!" when she saw Sara in the hall. So Sara stopped to talk, and the talk led to a few games of cribbage, which pleased Blanche.

"It's good to have company while Harvey's away. Did you wonder why you haven't met him yet? He's at a craft fair upstate. He'll be back tonight. I didn't have the energy to go with him. This has been such a hot summer, but now it's half over. I usually find my get-up-and-go comes back in September. But you won't like to see your vacation over so fast, will you!"

"It hasn't felt like vacation. When school was out in Yellow Creek, I had to stay home every day to help Gran, so I didn't even see my friends. This is all so new, so different up here, I haven't had time to think about school."

"That's wise. Do one day at a time. Now — you ought to run along and see what everyone's up to."

After a quick breakfast, Sara went exploring. Standing in the deserted living room, she heard hammering somewhere in the barn, and from outside she heard a dog's bark and the clatter of the goats' bells. From an open door at the far end of the large living area came the sound of music. She looked in and found Kyra's studio, which had big windows on three sides. On an easel by a north window was a large canvas. Kyra sat on a stool, staring first out the window and then at the canvas, which had a few slashes of green and gold and blue on it. She wore paint-stained carpenter's overalls.

Sara cleared her throat. "Excuse me, do you know where Richard is?"

"Hi, Sara! Come in." Kyra turned down the radio. "Richard is loading the wood-burning kiln. His work has been going better than mine." She waved at the canvas.

"What are you painting?"

"Usually I paint what I feel about what I see. I mean, it's basically landscape. But in terms of light and shapes. Not a-tree-is-a-tree-is-a-tree, if you know what I mean."

"I don't." Sara could see that Kyra was not going to be an easy person to figure out. Especially where her art was concerned.

"It's hard to explain, and even though I've been here since April, I haven't done anything I'd want to show you." Kyra was intense about her work. "I don't *feel* yet about New Hampshire. For the last few years I've been painting in Spain and on Crete. In both places the light strikes you down, it's so furious. It makes terrific shadows. I'm used to brilliant light and looking out over sea or plains for a horizon. I look out here and I'm lost. I never should have let Richard persuade me to come."

Sara wanted to ask where Richard and Kyra had met, how long they had known each other. But Kyra went on, "This is so different. Things don't have strong angles. They curve. They roll. The colors blend all together. Look how many greens you see out there." She shook her head; then she picked up her brush and, concentrating, seemed to forget Sara was there.

Sara wandered out and went down to the middle level of the barn, where Zeke and Ben were tearing out old partitions and preparing to put up walls. She stood there listening to the wrenching screech of tough wood being pried apart; Ben's singsong swearing when something wouldn't give; to the tympani of hammering; the ear-splitting yowl of planks being run through a power saw; the squeak of a planer; and the swishing sizzle of a sander spewing up clouds of dust. The two men were so absorbed that they didn't notice her.

The next floor, where Ben and Harvey Wicketts had their shops, was deserted. The door to Mr. Wicketts' shop was open, and Sara saw hundreds of tiny pieces of wood, like a giant jigsaw puzzle, scattered over his workbench. But she didn't want to explore without being invited.

On the lowest level Gabe was in the pottery, helping Richard load one of the electric kilns with the punch cups that hadn't been broken. Sara stood out of the way. Mickey, the long-eared, sway-bellied hound who always seemed to be within sight and sound of Gabe, lay in a breeze-buzzed spot by the door. The insides of his ears were veined and shiny, with the soft sheen of a mother-of-pearl shell. His side rose and fell with his breathing, but Sara had the feeling that he would rise up and roar if Fonzie came tippeting along.

"Sara, take this out and put it on the table by the wood-burning kiln." Her father held out a bowl that was coated with a gray slurry. It rested on a traylike circle of plaster. "Just hold onto the bat and you won't have to touch the pot. I've sprayed the glaze on and I want to fire it in the wood burner."

She clutched the bat and moved slowly, hoping there were

no obstacles to trip her. Her father followed, carrying a tray loaded with pots. Gabe too made frequent trips, bringing one large bowl at a time. Richard said, "Sara, if you and Gabe hand me things, I won't have to scramble in and out of the kiln."

Sara took a good look at the structure. The base was a large rectangle, up from which rose a shape that arched a little higher than Richard's head. It was formed of large yellow firebricks cemented together and was about twelve feet deep. At the back a brick chimney rose twenty feet in the air. Several feet up from the ground there was an opening in the front of the kiln into a tunnel that arched through the middle.

Richard climbed in and knelt in the tunnel. He could half turn and reach toward them when they handed him things, but it was uncomfortable, and turning was difficult. On each side of him, brushing his shoulders, were walls of firebricks that met the arch as it curved down. Between the inside walls and the outside walls were the fire boxes, their metal doors opening at the front of the kiln.

"Now, Gabe," Richard commanded, "hand me one of those saggers, if you can. They're heavy."

Gabe picked up one of the deep, flat-bottomed oval containers made of ceramic. He had to bend to the task, and it wasn't easy because of the sagger's weight and smoothness. He edged it in to Richard, who placed it at the back of the tunnel. "Now, Sara, hand me a set of cones — those four little ceramic spikes over there."

"What do they do?"

"Each of them melts at a different temperature. When I unload the kiln, I check the cones, and then I can tell how high the temperature went in each sagger. It's not always the

42

same in different parts of the kiln." Then he placed another sagger on top of that and filled it with two large pots.

After four tiers of saggers, Richard backed up a little toward the entrance and started another set of tiers. It was like slowly and fussily building a layer cake. When he had worked his way through the last tier, Richard covered the top sagger and placed the last set of cones on it.

It took him a long time to load the kiln, yet Sara stayed to help. She wanted to be as useful as Gabe, and she hoped her father realized that so far she hadn't dropped or cracked one pot. Richard bricked up the tunnel entrance, leaving one brick he could pull in and out easily. "That's my peephole, so I can look in and see that nearest set of cones. Then I'll see how hot it is — at least in the front of the kiln."

"How hot do you have to make it?"

"Cone nine. That's roughly twenty-five hundred degrees Fahrenheit. I'll start slow and let it muddle along until late in the day, and then we'll have a real stoking session. So thanks, kids, but I won't need any more help until then."

Gabe whistled up Mickey. "Want to go check on the goats with me?" he asked Sara.

Sara hesitated. She was pleased that Gabe wanted her company, but she wanted to talk with her father — not about anything in particular. Just to get reacquainted. "I'll see you later," she told Gabe.

She watched while her father started the fire in each of the fire boxes, coaxing them from sullen smoking to brisk burning each time he fed a few sticks in. He took off his shirt and, in between loadings, waited on the bench. Sara thought this might be a good time to ask him where he had met Kyra and how long he'd known her. He, however, gave a lecture on

43

pottery — from Mexican to Chinese porcelain — until he said he was hungry.

"Do you want me to bring you some lunch?" Sara asked.

"That's a nice thought. Very Saradipity." He smiled at her. It was like having the candle lit inside a jack-o'-lantern, for not only his eyes but his skin seemed to warm and glow. "How's it going? Have you made friends with Demetri and Kyra? With Gabe?"

"Demetri's made friends with Fonzie. They tipped me out of bed this morning. Kyra was painting so hard I didn't want to bother her."

"So she's painting! That's good news. She's been having a struggle."

"You are talking about me!" Kyra appeared, carrying a lunch basket. "My ears buzzed. Sara told you I painted big stripes on my canvas."

"No, I didn't — "

Kyra put her hand on Sara's arm. "I'm teasing. Will you have some cheese? Bread? Fruit? Goat's milk?"

"No thanks." The basket and its contents reminded Sara of traveling with her father, of the lunch baskets that had been opened on trains and in cars, on boats and in carts, and all the overheated cheese and tough bread of her childhood. She wanted a squushy, mushy liverwurst slathered with mayonnaise on springy white bread.

"See you." She approached the barn by the ladder to the deck. Would Gabe slither out of the tree? Or was he eating a lunch of bread and cheese near the goats on the hill? It would be great, she thought, if he had a bell around his neck, one with a special tone, so she'd know where he was, for Gabe intrigued her. She felt a kind of mystery about him, an importance of things different and unknown that no boy in Yellow Creek had ever projected. She stood in the cool shade of the deck thinking about Gabe, thinking how neat it would be to walk into school in September with such a gypsy-looking friend. She was sure half the girls in the school must be scheming over him.

With a whoop and a thud, Gabe let go of the rope and landed on the deck.

"I didn't even hear you coming down the hill!"

"You looked kind of spacey."

"I'm not spacey. I was thinking."

"What were you thinking about?"

Sara remembered Bethy-Sue's and Laura-Ellen's discovery that boys liked to talk about themselves. She took a chance and said, "You."

Gabe didn't seem particularly flattered, although he was curious about her thoughts. "Good or bad?"

"Why should I tell you?" Sara teased, yet the words sounded too sharp. They didn't have the breathy intimacy that Bethy-Sue had recommended. So she hastily added, "Good."

"You'd better. That's what Richard says makes group living work — the good things about people. I like your father, you know. I like him a lot. Better than I like my own father, that's for sure."

Sara remembered Richard's explanation of why Gabe had asked to move into the barn, that his father had been beating him up. She wondered if he would mention that. He didn't; he just added, "My family lives half a mile down the road. There's a lot of us, so I was glad to get out. I guess they don't even miss me."

Since that didn't seem to distress him, Sara couldn't think

of what to say. Nor did she want to discuss her own feelings about her father with him. As always, she was too uncertain of Richard, of his motives. She decided it would be more practical to ask about school and life in Martin's Corners.

They went along to the kitchen, and while Sara made sandwiches, Gabe answered her questions in a big-brotherly way. If he thought of Richard as a substitute father, he was apparently going to treat her as a substitute sister. Sara wasn't sure she liked that.

After supper Richard organized the kiln-stoking. He and Gabe handled one firing door and Ben and Zeke the other, while Sara and Kyra kept sticks of wood and bundles of twigs handy for them to grab. They also kept cans of ice-cold beer at the ready. Stoking was hot work.

On signal Gabe and Zeke pulled the iron doors wide open and Richard and Ben stuffed in the wood or the twig bundles. Then the others slammed the doors shut. They used iron pokers, with ends that Richard had forged, to catch the door handles. He and Ben wore asbestos gloves and long-sleeved shirts to protect themselves against flying sparks.

Sara found that standing within three or four feet of the kiln could be uncomfortable, and whenever the doors were opened, the heat pulsed out in waves. There was a roar and a crackle and sometimes loops of flame spilled out and only subsided as new logs were thrown into them.

Every fifteen minutes Richard opened the peephole to see how the cones stood. He kept a notebook for writing down the time. Everyone cheered when the first cone fell.

Half an hour later another cone fell. After that, despite stepping up the stoking, nothing happened. Richard had a pyrometer too — a gauge with a wire that led into the kiln and gave a rough measurement of the temperature inside. Each time the doors were opened and wood added, the temperature fell a little. It gained back slowly, but it didn't indicate the steady rise Richard hoped for. "This is the first time I've tried for cone nine. It may take some redesign and rebuilding to do such high firings." He kept making notes.

Sara was excited for the first hour or two. It was so different from anything she'd experienced around Yellow Creek. Kyra sat on the ground, leaning against the bench, with Demetri half awake in her arms. In between stokings, the men stood about. As the pace of the firing picked up, there was barely time for them to gulp something cold and wipe the sweat from their foreheads.

By midnight, as a current of clouds washed out the moon, it was dark as the depths of the sea. Sara thought they were all swimming in a film of heat. Each time the firing doors were yanked open, the men's bodies were strobed with brilliant light from the flames. The wood seemed to explode as it met the intense heat, and the coals sizzled down into the ash pits. From the chimney came a continual roar as a column of flame rose into the sky

It was flame such as Sara had never seen before — not dancing orange streaks with sequins of golden sparks, but heavy rods of ugly red fused with purple and blue streaks like bruises. It reached up, shaking and roaring and menacing the sky. Sara found herself backing away from the heat and the noise as if she, like a piece of wood thrown inside, might be consumed by the fire and go rocketing up the chimney, her scream of protest lost in the drumroll sound of the flames as she disappeared into the night sky as one small petal of ash.

She stepped back so quickly that she banged into Gabe,

47

who was picking up a cold drink. "Sorry! That fire — it's too much!"

"You're shaking. Are you scared?" Gabe asked.

"Yes. I am. A little."

"It's safe. The kiln won't blow up or anything. This is the hottest we've ever gotten it. I think it's great!" He took off his sweatband and wrung some drops of water out of it.

"It's great all right," Sara agreed, moving out of his way. "It's incredible!" But she didn't go as close as she had been before.

She watched Richard pull the brick out of the peephole and stand as close as he could without searing his face. Even from where she had retreated, she saw, by a quick glance at the peephole, that the light was so dazzling it seemed to have no color at all. She blinked, feeling as if it had stabbed her eyes.

"Yippy-dippy-do!" Richard's shout of triumph startled them. "Hey-hey-hey! Cone nine is down! We made it. We can wood-fire porcelains after all." He pulled Kyra into an exuberant hug. "We can fire with wood instead of electricity. I can save energy — and lose weight! — at the same time. I must have sweated off ten pounds."

"You do feel slippery." Kyra slid out of his embrace.

"You're losing a lot of heat up the chimney," Zeke observed. "If you could keep it in the kiln, you could cut the amount of wood you need and maybe even the length of time it takes to get to cone nine."

They looked and listened to the fire raging out of the chimney. "Good point," admitted Richard. "We could change the inside walls and lengthen the chimney. Well, Sara, what do you think of your old man now? No more the dry little guy who used to study and write about pots! Isn't your father a much more exciting person?"

"It's all fantastic!" Sara said. The intensity of the experience and her father's thrill in it were exciting, yet she felt that pillar of fire would be imprinted on her eyes and its unpitying roar would resound in her ears for a long time. And what about it made her father feel so high? The achievement of the firing? or the drama of the fire?

She looked at Gabe and saw that he felt triumphant too, especially as he had taken part in the creativity that went into the firing. Pots his hands had shaped from lumps of wet clay were going to emerge from the heat and the smoke of the kiln in a perfected state. Things that he had made would be transformed, and he could look at them with both wonder and pride. Sara yearned to share in such a profound experience.

Suddenly they all felt exhausted. Not even Demetri protested when Kyra carried him in to the barn. Sara was so tired that her canvas cot seemed to cradle her body in a comforting way, yet as she drifted toward sleep, she thought of asking Gabe to teach her how to throw a pot so she could surprise her father.

# 5

The scheme of learning to throw a pot so she could surprise her father lurked in Sara's mind. Over the next few days she often went to the pottery, hoping to find Gabe there alone and ask for his help. Her father always seemed to be there. It was the tourist season, and through the craft fairs and the League of New Hampshire Arts and Crafts shops, Bradford Earthforms was doing a flourishing business. Richard worked from daylight to twilight, mixing clay or glazes, throwing pots or turning them — which he explained as trimming and neatly footing their bottoms. "And don't ask me why you foot a bottom."

Sara hoped too that if she hung around long enough and watched hard enough, as a big blob of clay flowed into a thin-walled vase or bowl under her father's caressing hands, she'd be prepared to do as well when she finally tried it. It looked like such a simple thing to do. So far, her father had been too busy meeting orders to take time to teach her anything, despite his remark to Gabe, before her arrival, that she might help in the pottery. Or perhaps he was apprehensive that if she spent a lot of time there, Fonzie would too — and he wasn't to be trusted.

Sara discovered her father was aware of how often she

dropped by, when he teased her about it. "What are you so interested in here, Sara? The pots? or me? or Gabe?"

Her first reaction was flustered discomfort, especially since Gabe could hear. And she didn't want to let on what her secret project was. Luckily she could change the subject by delivering a message. "Harvey wants to know if you need anything from Rochester and if he could borrow the truck to drive there. He'll take me to look for a secondhand bed and Blanche will come to help me buy material to make a spread and curtains."

"Take the truck. And here — " Richard pulled some crumpled bills out of his jeans' pocket. "I hope that's enough for a bed and a mattress. Good luck! Oh, and as you go upstairs, will you ask Ben to come down and lend me a hand? I need his help to move some things."

Within the first few days, Sara had discovered there was a pattern of dependence under the seemingly separate lives they all led. She found out because her role became that of a messenger. Kyra, the cook, would ask Sara to find Zeke, the gardener, to tell her what was ready to harvest — for supper or for the freezer. Zeke, the woodcarver, would ask her to find Harvey, the miniature-maker, and remind him to pick up some wood from a friend in Martin's Corners. Harvey, the errand-runner, would send Sara to tell Blanche to wait for him to come back so he could help her with any canning or freezing. Sara was grateful that Blanche usually provided a rest area, a pause for a game of cribbage.

This time, as Sara carried the message from Richard, Ben asked, "How's it going? Are you finding enough things to do?"

"Plenty! All of you keep me running, taking messages back and forth!"

Ben laughed. "We thought of putting in an intercom, but I'd rather have a word from you than from a squawk box."

Sara enjoyed the trip with Harvey and Blanche, who were old hands at browsing and bargaining in secondhand shops. They found a small brass bed frame and a decent mattress. The only problem was in buying material. Sara's choices and Blanche's choices were so different.

"Of course it's your room," Blanche admitted, "and if you want such an ordinary little flower pattern, that's your choice." She turned away reluctantly from a bolt of cloth displaying vivid jungle birds amid overwhelming blossoms.

"I like those little flowers," Sara insisted. She'd found a design that reminded her of the daisies and buttercups on the hill by the barn.

Sara had thrown some of the material over the new bed, when Kyra came into her room to see what she'd bought. "That brightens up your room handsomely, but you need some pictures on your walls. Let me see what would look good — "

Sara expected her to bring a painting. Instead, Kyra brought matted photographs. "I started out as a photographer, and if I don't get my painting together soon, I'll go back to it." She gave Sara two color enlargements, one of children playing in a park fountain and one of a windmill with great white sails against an intense blue sky. A mustached, bearded man sat on the ground in front of the windmill, looking defiantly at the camera.

"That's Richard!" Sara said.

"That's how I met him. I asked him to move so I could take that angle of the windmill, and he wouldn't budge. He said every picture should have a person to give it human interest and the right scale. I told him he was an interfering, opinionated nut, and we've been arguing over photographs and paintings ever since."

"When did you meet him?"

"It must have been about three years ago. I was going to Spain for a few months, and he was looking for a house, so I rented him mine. When I came back to Crete, he offered to find another place, but there was lots of room and I didn't mind his company, especially when he enjoyed Demetri so much."

Sara had a question she had to ask. "What about Demetri's father? Did he live there too?"

"No. I split with Georgios when Demetri was six months old. I grew up in Florida — in Tarpon Springs. My grandparents came there from Greece years ago. Georgios was a distant cousin. He came to visit when I was seventeen. He was so handsome and I thought living in Greece would be glamorous. So I married him and went off to Athens, and by the time I was nineteen and had Demetri, I didn't want to be just a housewife and a mother. Especially as my husband made all the decisions and gave all the orders. He couldn't understand my wanting to go out of the house — to be a photographer. I couldn't understand his male chauvinism, so we split up. I took Demetri and went to Crete. Then along came Richard — "

Which led to Sara's next question — the one she didn't dare put into words: Why don't you and Richard get married?

Unaware of what was in Sara's mind, Kyra went on, "Your father is a lot of fun. I get a kick out of the way he enjoys people and places and doing all kinds of things. It's been fascinating to see how he's changed from a ceramic historian into a potter. I couldn't believe he'd be so different — even to shaving off his beard — in the six months he spent setting up the pottery and the barn before I came over."

"Why did he come here? Instead of doing pottery on Crete? Why did he shave off his beard?"

"You're as full of whys as Demetri! Richard inherited the barn. Didn't he tell you? He'd never heard of the place until his great-uncle's lawyer wrote him that he owned it. So he had to come and see and it took just one look to inspire him to — all this. And his beard? I think it was a bit symbolic. New life; new face."

"Do you think he's settled down?" Sara pretended to concentrate on putting the photographs up on the wall with push-pins.

"Who knows? He's a restless man."

"I remember."

"Of course you do! According to Richard, you lived in ten different countries before you were seven years old."

"I don't remember much about any of them except a lot of packing and unpacking and never being sure of how to ask for the bathroom."

"It's too bad you weren't old enough to enjoy it. I love to move from country to country, painting and photographing. As long as they're warm countries. I can't stand the cold. Richard keeps telling me he wasn't cold living here last winter, but I don't believe him."

Sara stood back to look at the photographs. "Thank you for the pictures. I'm glad to have one of Richard, even if he does look mad."

Kyra laughed. "He never stays mad long. He's a charming man. If he weren't, I wouldn't be here."

As each day spun along, Sara tested new threads in the web. She liked to watch Harvey in his shop. He worked so quietly she could hear his breathing. He used tweezers to pick up a tiny latch or a hinge or a delicate molding he had carved and, placing it carefully, glued it to a piece of minute furniture. Sometimes he asked Sara for help. "You have a steady hand. Blanche offers to help but she wobbles too much." He hummed as he worked too — tuneless buzzing sounds like committee reports of satisfied bees. Sara was always surprised to find an hour had slipped away before she knew it.

After Zeke showed her how the three worst weeds looked — the branchy, tiny-flowered chickweed, the belligerent pokeweed, and tough pigweed, she sometimes helped him with the weeding. She didn't have the patience, though, to transplant carrots. The clumps of feathery seedlings stuck to her fingers and were so fragile that they broke when she tried to separate them. She didn't like it when worms pulsed against her fingers and clung when she tried to shake them off.

"Never mind the transplanting," Zeke told her. "That's fussy stuff. But you can weed any time. You do that like a pro!" She was pleased too when Ben put her to work rubbing antiquing stain on some chairs and told her she did it just right.

Sara spent a lot of time with Blanche as well, for it eased a guilty feeling she had over leaving Gran, even though that couldn't be helped. Sometimes they played cribbage and sometimes Sara watched Blanche crochet her flaming afghan squares. "Could you teach me to knit?" Sara asked. "I want to make a sweater for Richard. For Christmas."

Blanche had plenty of yarn and pattern books. Sara chose a sweater with a V-neck and cable-stitch front that she thought

55

would look handsome on her father. Blanche patiently demonstrated knitting and purling and making cables, and Sara tried to get the stitches right, but the painfully knitted results were knobby and misshapen. Each time she ripped it back, the yarn looked dirtier and more tortured.

"Try a scarf first, dearie," Blanche advised.

"No, I'll start all over once more." Sara didn't like to be defeated. Everyone in the barn made things. Even Demetri hammered pieces of wood together and painted them, and Richard told him to call them constructions, adding, "Not bad for a kid."

"Then take some fresh yarn. The life is pulled out of that stuff. And relax. Knit with the yarn; don't fight with it."

The August heat helped Sara give in. "Maybe you're right. I'll try a scarf for Richard. Tomorrow. When it's a little cooler. Want a game of cribbage?"

"Not right now." Blanche looked at the digital clock on the bureau. "How do you like that blinking thing? I found it in a flea market. At my stage of life I need one that will wink, not tock." Blanche enjoyed making puns. "Get it? Not talk!" Her yarn rolled off her lap and ran away when she laughed.

Sara fished the balls out from under the bed and handed them to her.

"Time for my beauty nap," Blanche explained. "It's too hot to think. You could win every game today."

Blanche looked sweaty and her breath was short. It was a sizzling day. Even on the top floor of the barn, which was usually breeze-swept, the air seemed dead.

Sara retreated to her room and put on her shortest shorts and her tank-top T-shirt. She leaned out the window that viewed the hillside. The goats were resting in the shade, occasionally twitching an ear to shake off a fly. Gabe wasn't with them. He was probably down in the pottery.

It was unusually quiet in the barn. Kyra and Demetri took naps after lunch, a custom they carried over from hot Mediterranean noontimes. "Besides," said Kyra, "with the sun overhead and no shadows, the light isn't good for painting. So I rest my eyes and my mind."

Sometimes Richard came to nap with them. Once Sara had gone by their open door and seen them on the double mattress on the floor, all asleep. Kyra was in the middle, with her arms around Demetri, and Richard's head snugged into the back of her neck, his arm resting along her thigh. Sara had walked by quickly, yet she noticed how contented they looked; how they seemed to belong to each other even as they each dreamed differently within themselves. She wondered what would happen if she'd gone in and said, "Move over. Make room for me too."

They probably would lazily have made room for her, without a word — and it wouldn't have proved a thing. Taking naps was not a permanent solution.

Ben had gone off early that morning on a custom cabinet job and Zeke had taken fresh vegetables to a farmer's market near Lake Winnepesaukee. Sara felt lazy; she stretched out on her bed to read and fell asleep.

A crash of thunder woke her. Gran had always said noise was just that — noise — and it couldn't hurt you and you had less chance of being struck by lightning than hit by a car. As the storm roiled around, echoing through the valley and crackling over the hill, Sara thought of Gran's pronouncement about the noise of thunder and tried to read and ignore it.

The storm, however, soon sounded like a competition for

percussion players, full of drumrolls and fancy paradiddles, and at its peak, a clashing of cymbals, which sent her leaping off the bed and down the hall.

She rushed into the open door of the Wicketts' room, only to discover Blanche peacefully snoring on her more-than-half of the bed, and Harvey, in jeans and no shirt, his chest stippled with white hair, resting in the patch of space left. He was reading. He looked up at Sara and winked. He beckoned her in and pointed to the chaise.

She shook her head and left. She was used to Harvey the miniature-maker; Harvey the harvest-helper; Harvey the grandfather-type who loved to tell stories to Demetri. It was the first time she'd barged in on Harvey the husband, and she was embarrassed.

Further down the hall was the door to the tiny room where a ladder led up into the cupola topping the barn. Just as Sara ran by it, there was a horrendous noise, as if a whole display of fireworks were exploding in that one small space. There were thuds and crackles and sizzles and bangs.

Sara yelled and ran. Getting to the pottery was like running an obstacle race — down a flight here, through a hall there, down another flight, through a storeroom, down a set of steep stairs to Ben's workshop, and finally down the open-tread stairs to the bottom of the barn. She was almost breathless when she rushed into the shop.

Her father was about to pour water into powdered clay in the drum of an electric mixing machine.

"The barn's been hit! The cupola got zapped."

Richard righted the bucket and dashed for the stairs. "Bring more buckets!"

Gabe deserted his wheel and grabbed two plastic pails,

thrusting them at Sara; taking two more, he started after Richard.

"Hey!" Sara shouted. "Aren't you going to fill the buckets?"

"Sure. Up there!"

"Oh." Of course that made sense. By the time her father reached the fifth floor, he would have spilled most of the water he was carrying. Where Richard had leaped into action, she saw that Gabe had stopped to think about it.

When, with her heart banging in her chest, she reached the top floor, the door to the cupola room was open. A blue-gray haze floated out . . . and a sulphurous odor came with it. Her father was laughing over the small amount of water left in his pail.

Harvey was chuckling too. He had grabbed an antique china pitcher, part of an old commode set, and discovered there weren't any flames to put out even before Richard arrived. Kyra had come running with a broom.

Demetri capered, holding his nose. Blanche leaned in her doorway with her hand cupped over the general vicinity of her heart. Gabe had filled his buckets just in case. Sara put hers down.

"Glory!" exclaimed Richard. "That was close. We're lucky it was only noise and smoke. No flames. This barn could be a disaster if it caught fire."

"Why?" Sara asked. "The timbers are so big it would take hours for them to burn through."

"And we'd be trying to put the fire out with buckets and a pitcher — filled under a faucet."

"You need tons of water to put out a big fire," Gabe said. "There aren't any hydrants way out here."

"Well, we're lucky," said Richard. "There must be a lightning rod on top of the cupola or there would have been flames for sure. You heard the whack when it struck, Sara. From the smell, it did make a damn strong fizzle-sizzle."

"A fizzle-sizzle!" Demetri was intrigued by the words. He spread his arms and planed along the hall, banking and yelling, "Fizzle-sizzle."

Kyra wiped her hair back from her forehead. "That was scary. Thank God we don't often have thunder as ghastly as that on Crete."

"What about all those Greek gods who stormed around?" Richard laughed as he put his arm around her. "The Greeks were into thunder and lightning long before anyone else."

"Maybe. But my house is close to the ground. Not way up in the air like this."

"Are you complaining?"

"Only about being frightened."

"I'll stay with you till you calm down." They wandered along to their room.

What about me? Sara thought. He could have asked if I was frightened too. She saw Harvey turn anxiously to look for Blanche, who was no longer in the doorway. "Storms like that sure do rev up the ticker. I'll rest with Blanche a bit. It's still too hot to work." With the Wicketts comforting each other too, Sara felt very left out.

Then Gabe said, "The pottery's the coolest place to be. Want to come down there, Sara?" He gathered the pails.

"Sure. I'll bring my book and read."

"Never mind the book. You can talk to me. The radio's full of static."

"Oh, thanks! Just don't expect a talk show."

60

They detoured through the kitchen for some glasses of switchel, a drink Harvey made by the gallon and kept in the refrigerator. "It's an old Yankee treat," he had explained. "It kept the haymakers from keeling over with heat exhaustion." It was made of a potent mix of molasses, vinegar, and powdered ginger diluted with water. Sara thought when she first tasted it that a little went a very long way, especially when she saw Harvey add oatmeal and eggs to it and drink it for breakfast. Now, in the muggy heat, it seemed restoring and delicious.

It was delicious too, Sara discovered, being close to Gabe as they sat at the kitchen table sipping switchel. Sara became aware of everything about him, from the swift blink of his eyelashes to the sound of his breathing. She wished Yellow Creek was near enough so she could phone Bethy-Sue and Laura-Ellen and tell them about him, but it would be difficult to claim him as a boy friend when Gabe only seemed to be acting brotherly.

They watched the last wisps of dirty cloud disappearing over the hills. Gabe splashed his face with water that ran so cold into the kitchen sink. "Let's go."

Sara was surprised to find her father and Demetri already in the shop. They hadn't stayed upstairs with Kyra for long. Demetri sat on a high stool at one end of the wedging table, poking holes into a lump of clay. He broke some off and wriggled a snake out between his hands. Sara pulled up a stool and sat, watching the others.

Her father switched on the mixing machine. It thumped around, with its gigantic beaters turning the water and powdered clay into a mucky mess. "Clay's funny," he told Sara. "It has to be just right — not too wet and not too dry — to work well. After it's mixed, I put this soppy clay into these drying bats. They're made of plaster and they suck water out of the clay so it dries faster."

"How long does it take?"

"A day or two." He went to an old icebox and brought out a plastic bag of clay and took a large chunk from it. It seemed stiff when he broke it off. He took it to the wedging table, where a thin wire angled down from a bar above the table to a screweye at its edge. He sliced the clay on the wire and then banged the halves onto a slab of polished granite that topped the table. He picked up the pieces, slapped them together, sliced them apart, and whacked them down again. He did it quickly but with clout. Slice, whack, wham; slice, whack, wham. Over and over.

"What are you doing that for?"

"To get out the air bubbles and make sure all of the clay has the same consistency. It's called wedging. Kyra says when she feels frustrated, she kneads bread dough. This works just as well. Maybe better, eh, Gabe?"

"It's better than a punching bag." He picked up a hunk of clay and wedged too. "Sometimes I even pretend —" Slice. "This clay —" Whack. "Is my old man." Wham.

She watched as Richard broke off a piece of the clay he'd been wedging, twisted it in his fingers, and found that it suited him. He took a round plaster bat and set it onto the metal disc in the center of his potter's wheel. Then he carefully smacked a hunk of clay onto the center of the bat, patting it into a cone shape. He sat in front of the wheel, sprinkled the clay with water to make it more slippery, and set the wheel turning with a foot control. As the clay spun he firmed it, teasing it up into a solid mass under his hands.

Sara noticed how big his hands were. She could barely see the clay under his fingers. Then the cone grew, springing up almost magically, as his hands defined the shape, up and up.

"Now!" Richard said, sensing Sara was watching him. "Look at this." He made a dent in the center with his thumbs. The dent became a hole, and the hole opened out into the clay as it spun. "There's the inside of the pot." He stopped the wheel, took his hands off the clay, leaned back, and squinted at the shape. Then he set the wheel turning again. He kept one hand in the pot and held a small piece of shaped wood that he called a rib on the outside of it. He pulled the pot taller and taller so its walls grew thinner and thinner. He made it flare out wide a few inches from the base, brought it in, and then out. Again he stopped the wheel and leaned back to study the outside shape. Then, in the rim at the top, he pulled out a flared lip. "Can you guess what this is?"

"Some kind of bottle?"

"Not quite. I'll put a handle on it when it's dried and what-ho! You'll have a pitcher — like Harvey's antique one. I'll make you a washbowl to go with it. Or you can make the bowl yourself. Want to try throwing one?"

Here it was — a confrontation Sara had hoped to avoid by some practice sessions with Gabe. She thought of the sweater that was turning into a scarf. Maybe she could avoid failure if she started small. "How about if I make an ashtray? Like Demetri's doing with his coils?"

"I'm not making ashtrays." Demetri glared at her. "These are turtles. Sleeping turtles."

"Excuse me!"

"Come over here." Richard put a clean bat onto a wheel and handed her a lump of clay. "Whack it down on the bat.

Make sure it's in the middle. Centering at the start is the secret of a successful pot."

"My hands aren't big enough. You and Gabe have huge hands."

"Throwing takes steadiness and skill. Not strength or big hands."

Sara took her courage literally in her hands as she whopped her clay onto the bat. As she stepped on the control, the wheel came alive. She felt the clay under her fingers, pushing at her, as if it were trying to throw her hands off.

"Get your hands around the base more. Make sure it's firm."

She tried. At first the plaster tickled against the soft edges of her hands. As the wheel went faster, friction developed and the plaster roughed her skin. It felt as if her hands were burning, but Sara kept trying to force the clay into a cone shape. She knew Gabe was watching her. That made it even more important that she succeed. "Oh, please, sweet Jesus," she prayed silently, remembering the kind of praying she heard at Gran's church. "Let this lump of clay, this insignificant bit of dirt You put here on earth —" In her head she could hear someone calling out "Amen" and "Praise the Lord." "Let it rise up and turn itself into a pot!"

When she realized what she was praying about, though, she felt silly. Did it really matter to her father — or to Gabe — whether she could throw a pot or not? Or did it only matter to her?

The more she tried, the worse she felt. Her clay lump didn't rise up. It spread out. She stopped the wheel to stare at her mess.

"Having a problem?" Richard asked.

"All I'm doing is making a pancake."

"I've never seen anyone do that before!" Richard couldn't help laughing, just when Sara wanted some sympathy. "You must have leaned on it instead of holding it up." He took the bat with its flat mass off the wheel and handed her one with another ball of clay.

"I don't think I'm meant to be a potter."

"Are you giving up after one try?"

Sara wanted to say, "Yes, I am." She wanted to get up from the wheel with dignity and leave before Gabe and Demetri remarked on her disaster, but her father stood there, waiting to help, and he did look sympathetic now that he saw she was troubled.

"It's not easy the first time, but once you get the hang of it, it's a powerful feeling, isn't it, Gabe?"

"Right!" Gabe agreed.

Sara sighed and adjusted the bat on the wheel. Her nose itched and she rubbed it, leaving a slimy brown streak like a snail's trail on her face. Once again she bent over the whirling wheel, clutching the clay, and again, the clay did not rise up, even though her fingers ached from urging it. Her cone began to shorten and spread out.

"Try putting your thumbs into the center and see what happens," said her father.

She tried and at least that worked. The hole grew wider as she pulled her thumbs apart, but the shape grew shorter and shorter. Finally she stopped the wheel.

"It looks like the ashtrays we made in Scouts by melting old phonograph records," she said with disgust. "And my hands feel as if they were burning."

"Rinse them off and let me see."

Sara rinsed them in the sink and inspected them. The soft edges of her palms and the sides of her little fingers were bright pink, and there were raw spots at the knuckles.

"Good God!" Richard exclaimed. "You've got blisters from trying to throw a pot. That's impossible!"

"No, it isn't impossible. I did it."

She could see her father was torn between plain amazement and amazement mixed with pity. She wished he did not have such a readable face.

"Never mind, Saradipity," he said. "You'll be great at a zillion other things. You'd better put something on those blisters, though." He turned away to adjust the clay-mixer.

Great at what! wondered Sara. Her father admired people who could make things. They were the ones he wanted around him. Sara noted that Demetri had a whole fleet of funny turtles and that the pot Gabe whirled on the wheel was now so high it hid his arm right up to the elbow. As she left the shop, she heard Richard's shout of praise to Gabe. She was thrilled that Gabe had made something beautiful. His talent made him seem even more wonderful. She would write Bethy-Sue and Laura-Ellen all about him — how handsome he was; how artistic. She'd write tomorrow. When her hands stopped stinging.

Yet her father's unstinted praise ringing out to Gabe had sliced into her feelings about herself as keenly as the wedging wire severed the clay. How could she ever accomplish anything that would make Richard sing her praises, that would let him see her as something more than his inept daughter?

66

# 6

"You could be a big help this morning, Sara, if you'd pick a few quarts of blueberries." Blanche rested at the kitchen table with her second cup of coffee. "When Gabe brought the berries for the pie I made yesterday he said the high bushes are blue with berries. It's cooler today, and I feel like making jam. Have you ever made jam?"

"No. But I could pick berries." Sara saw no problem with such a simple task. "If I knew where they are. Near the barn? In the woods?"

"In the woods. You'll have to ask Gabe to tell you where."

Asking Gabe was no problem either. Sara hurried to the pottery, where her father and Gabe were busy at their humming wheels. She waited until Gabe was satisfied with the shape of a small vase. "Blanche needs four quarts of blueberries to make jam. I'll pick them, but I don't know where to find them. She said you'd know."

"Sure. You go up the hill, past the goats, and take the path along the ridge. You look for a big boulder about twice as tall as Richard —"

"Gabe," Richard interrupted, "how about helping Sara

pick berries? It's a dazzler of a day. Much too great to spend it here in the dim of the pottery."

"Okay." Gabe rinsed his hands in the water barrel and wiped them on his jeans. He looked at Sara's tank top, shorts, and sandals. "You better wear jeans and sneakers and a long-sleeved shirt. The mosquitoes can really bug you in the woods."

"Take some bug spray," Richard suggested.

"That stuff is full of chemicals," Gabe objected.

"Maybe. But we don't have rancid bear fat like the Indians used."

"They may have smelled worse, but I bet they lived longer," Gabe said. Sara realized that even though he admired her father, he wasn't shy about standing up to him. She went to change her clothes. When she met him on the deck, she found that he had assembled two plastic buckets with lids for each of them to carry. He also handed her a smaller pail on a rope. "You tie that around your waist, and then you have both hands free to pick. It goes a lot faster that way."

He set out, hiking up the hill with long steps. Mickey bounced at his heels. Sara determined to keep up, and she was out of breath by the time they reached the goats. Gabe checked the tethers and started on.

Sara followed along the path. She wanted to talk to Gabe, to find out what he liked to do when he wasn't working for her father, and what he thought about things. Any things. She wanted him to know her better, to want to stop and talk with her when they bumped into each other around the barn. He always seemed too busy to bother, except at mealtimes when everyone talked. Gabe walked so fast and the path was so narrow, she'd have to save her breath until they stopped to pick.

They had walked for about ten minutes when Gabe pointed to a great glacier-scratched boulder shaped like a whale's jaw. "That's the landmark. The swamp is to the left." He led the way through a tangle of underbrush.

"Are there snakes?"

"Why? Are you afraid of snakes?"

"Yes."

"That's silly. The black snakes around here are probably afraid of you."

"Any snake would make me jump. A cobra nearly bit me once. Mother found it by my bed and grabbed me up. Richard killed it." The memory still made Sara shudder.

"Wow! A cobra! How did he kill it?"

"I don't remember." She didn't want to remember.

"Well, there are no cobras here, and the swamp is dry in July. It's only wet enough in the spring for the bushes to do well. See how high they grow? You have to reach up sometimes to pick." He set his pails in a convenient spot and began picking, both hands at once, dropping the berries into the pail tied to his waist.

Sara set her buckets down and picked. For a while they worked without talking. The only sounds were the berries plinking into the pails; twigs crunching under their feet as they moved around the bushes; Mickey's eager snuffing nearby in the woods; and some birds calling "Phoebe! Phoe-bee!" Now and then Sara popped a sun-tinged berry into her mouth, tasting first the spicy tang and then the sweetness. She was a steady picker, although not as speedy as Gabe, and before long she tipped the berries from her pail into one of the buckets. Gradually the buckets were filled, without their needing to explore beyond the swamp.

Gabe straightened up and stretched. "Look at that sky."

Sara looked. It was brilliant. Cloudless. "What about it?"

"I never used to think about the sky. I mean, I knew if it was cloudy or sunny or rainy. The other day Richard and I were in the yard loading the wood burner and he said, 'Look at that blue in that sky. It's so intense. It's like a shout!' Just like that. Looking at a sky and coming out with what he thought about it. So — I've been really looking at the sky, at a lot of things he's talked about. You're lucky to have a man like Richard for a father."

Sara was walking ahead of Gabe, and she stopped so suddenly that Gabe bumped into her. "What makes you think I'm so lucky?" She was annoyed that anyone could think a girl who hadn't lived in the same house with her father for four years was all that lucky to have him for a father, and she spoke so abruptly that she sounded angry.

Gabe was surprised. "Well — aren't you? He's done all these interesting things. Lived in all these crazy places. He knows such fantastic stuff —"

"So? Look at the men who climb Mount Everest or spend a year at the South Pole or something. He's never done anything famous."

"So who needs to be famous?" They came to the boulder, and Gabe put his buckets down. He knew the contours of the boulder well, where to wedge his toes, where to grip with his fingers. He hauled himself up onto it and reached out to Sara. "Come on up."

"Sure." She found a toehold and, with Gabe's help, scrambled onto the slope of the rock. They climbed a few feet to the top and sat, dangling their legs over its steep side. Its height brought them up among the tops of the scrub pines, and there was enough of a breeze to cool their faces. Gabe whipped off his shirt. Sara wished she could do the same. She unbuttoned the neck of her shirt and rolled up the sleeves.

Gabe lifted his face toward the sun and shut his eyes, but he was still thinking about her father. "You must have had a great time, being in all those terrific places with Richard. He's told such funny stories about living in Japan and Iran and India."

"So he thought things were funny!"

"Didn't you?"

"I don't remember things being funny. I mean, Richard tried to make picnics out of traveling on trains and buses and boats and make parties out of being in weird places. But sometimes my mother and I lived in a cold room in a poor village for days while he'd be off at some monastery on a mountain or taking a trip on horseback or camel to see some tribes' special way of firing or decorating pots. He'd be having adventures and getting to the unusual out-of-the-way places no one else had studied, while my mother would be trying to teach me English and arithmetic. Or find ways to amuse me. She taught me how to fold birds and animals out of paper and how to cut shapes out of potatoes or even roots or squashes to make prints with them. But Richard didn't seem to understand that my mother didn't think living that way, and teaching me to make paper birds better than I could do long division, was the right way to educate me. She worried, too — about the dirt and diseases and danger. Things like that never concerned him at all."

"I can't imagine Richard being afraid of anything. Not if he could kill a cobra."

"He was great at the dramatic things. But getting sick from

bad food isn't dramatic. My mother was sicker than she let him know. She only kept going because she thought my father was the most wonderful man in the world. And he did love her. I know he did. She was very beautiful. They were tremendously in love —"

Sara sat, remembering. She remembered watching them when they seemed to have forgotten her, when they saw only each other. She remembered how bewildered her father had been when her mother died. "He couldn't believe it that mother died while he'd only been away for four days. He came back and she was dead. Richard was so angry and I thought he felt it was my fault somehow. Now I suppose he was angry at her being where there wasn't the right doctor or the right medicine. I remember his shouting and pounding his fists on the wall. He frightened me. You know, he yells when he's upset. Like the punch bowl and Fonzie."

"He had a reason to yell. I mean — when your mother died. My father yells and carries on over everything. He always thinks someone's cheating him or putting him down."

"Is that why you left home? Because he yells?"

"I could stand that. I always shut my head off when he starts to holler. And he knows it. It drives him wild. My older brothers did that too. Giles and Alphonse. They wouldn't answer him. He'd get so mad he'd punch them out. He's thin but he's strong and he uses his belt. He knocked Giles down the stairs once. Giles left the next day. He didn't finish school. And my father knocked Alphonse out one night in the barn and left him there. Unconscious. Alphie got pneumonia and nearly died. He left as soon as he could walk out the door. He didn't finish school either."

"Did he hit you?" Sara couldn't imagine Gabe making any-

72

one mad enough to hit him, not with those dark appealing eyes.

"A lot. The first time I met Richard, when he came to buy the goats, I couldn't see out of one eye and my face was all red and purple welts from Papa's beating up on me. I have four younger sisters — Yvonne, Elise, Annette, and Jean-Marie, and a little brother, Francie. And Mama is expecting another. That's another reason I wanted to leave. The house isn't big enough. It's all girls and babies, and my mother's too tired to take care of any of it. If Richard hadn't let me stay at the barn, I would have run away from Martin's Corners like my brothers did."

"Do they ever come home?"

"No. Giles is out near San Francisco. He sent a card last Christmas. Alphie's in the army in Germany. Papa thinks that's great. He says the army will make a man out of Alphie."

"Was your father in the army?"

"No. He grew up in Quebec Province and his father wanted him to be a priest. Priests are important in those little towns and every family wants one son to be a priest. He stuck it out in a seminary for a year and he hated it. He ran away and came to New Hampshire. I think the seminary training is why he sounds so stuffy when he speaks to people he doesn't know. Sort of phony polite."

"What does he do for a living?"

"He sells stuff. He sells wood and chickens and eggs and goats and lambs. When he feels like it. He's never kept a job for long because he drinks and then does something stupid and gets fired. Or he gets violent. If you think Richard yells and carries on, you should see my father. And he has a memory like an elephant and he broods. He can belt you in September for something you said in May. Believe me, it's a lot more peaceful to live with your father at the barn."

Sara shifted her position away from an uncomfortable bump in the rock, and her bare arm brushed Gabe's. He didn't move, and she let her arm rest against him not sure whether the prickles of dizziness dancing through her came from her skin touching his or from the dizziness of sitting at the edge of the boulder, as she glanced down onto the crowns of bushes below. She knew Blanche was waiting for the berries, but she didn't want to move. She glanced up at the sweep of sky and kept her face toward the sun, just as Gabe was doing, and a vermillion glow crept under her eyelids.

"We should go back," Gabe said. "Richard will need help loading the kiln this morning."

"I know. Blanche needs the berries. We'll go in a minute. You don't take much time off. You work hard."

"I like it. I mean, I like the kind of work at the barn. Making pots and glazing and firing. I hated the work my father made me do. Splitting and stacking wood — cords of it. Or killing hens and gutting them and plucking them."

"Yuck!" Sara remembered her mother having to kill a hen — somewhere in a hot climate on a hot day — and how smelly a process it was.

"Or cleaning eggs. That's cruddy work too. I'll never go back there to live! So I better get a move on or Richard will think I'm goofing off."

"No he won't. He told you to pick berries."

"And we've done it. Come on!" Gabe stood up and pulled his shirt over his head. Sara rose reluctantly. It was strange to stand taller than the scrubby trees and to look down on two chickadees chattering on a branch below. She watched Gabe

74

step off down the slant of the rock, until he reached a place where he could jump to the pine-needle-covered ground. She didn't have the courage to walk right down the rock that way, sort of pitched out into space. She turned and backed down, hoping Gabe wouldn't laugh at her. He didn't and he held out his hand when she jumped off the rock. She thought she would always remember that moment — the rush through the air, the clasp of his hand, and the scent of pine needles spiced by the sun. If only they both hadn't had to carry the berry buckets, perhaps he would have held her hand as they walked home. Sara hoped so. She hoped Blanche would want to make a lot of jam in the next few weeks, so they could go berry picking again.

One afternoon of making the jam, however, used up Blanche's energy and Sara's enthusiasm for hanging around the kitchen stirring steaming batches of berries. She did take pleasure, though, when the jars had cooled, in putting labels on them: BLUEBERRY JAM BY BLANCHE AND SARA 1981. And she took pride in Blanche's announcement at supper. "Sara and I accomplished a lot today. We put up twenty-four jars of blueberry jam."

"I'd like to send some to Gran," Sara said.

"Bring a few jars down to the pottery," her father told her, "and we'll put in a jam jar to go with them and pack them all up in those plastic peanuts so they won't break."

After supper she wrote to Bethy-Sue and Laura-Ellen and told them what a wonderful day she'd had. Richard even remarked on how contented Sara looked and how pleased he was at her helping Blanche. Sara smiled. Her daily encounters with her father seemed to be going smoothly. Fonzie had learned to keep out of the way. She had pleased her father with an accomplishment of her own, and she could look forward to seeing Gabe every day.

Several days later she was lingering over her breakfast when Richard walked in. "Saradipity! Come to Martin's Corners with me and run errands." He stood there with his usual ready-to-take-off stance, offering the trip as if it were a great adventure and the errands he needed help with were only incidental.

"Take me too!" Demetri jumped at Richard and twined his legs around him.

"We'll see what your mother says, Demi. We should go by the school," Richard reminded Sara. "You have to register. Let's go. You look great just the way you are."

"You want me to register for school looking like this?" Sara wore blue short shorts and one of the T-shirts Kyra had designed for all of them to wear to promote the pottery. They had EARTHFORMS in brown letters set against the orange shape of a flame. Sara felt particularly formless in the one she wore because it wasn't hers. It was Gabe's. She had extracted it from the communal wash, knowing it was too big for her, yet relishing it because it had clung to Gabe's torso. She wished she'd discovered it before it had been washed. She was waiting for Gabe to try fitting into hers and complain.

"What's wrong with advertising Earthforms?" Richard asked. "I'll put mine on too, by jolly!"

"Oh please don't. I mean —"

"You mean it's hard enough to go to another school without coming in freaky, accompanied by a freaky father?"

Sara looked at him in surprise. How did he know how she felt? Then she wondered if he was thinking more of the impression he'd make himself than how it might affect her. "I'll go change."

Upstairs she met Gabe. "Hey!" He caught her arm and twirled her around. "That shirt's too big for you and the one I got out of the wash is too small for me."

"They could have been mixed up in the wash," Sara suggested.

"Come on, that's mine. I'm going to town with Richard, and I want to wear mine and give Earthforms a boost." He stood there, bare-chested, in his jeans and sneakers, apparently waiting for her to strip off his shirt and hand it over. He held out her shirt. "Aren't you going to swap?"

As she wasn't wearing anything under her shirt, she couldn't strip then and there. She felt flushed and stupid. "Oh, sure!" She grabbed the shirt he was waving in front of her. "Give me a minute to change."

She'd told her father she'd wear something else, but now she wanted to look like Gabe, like a matched set. In her room she impatiently pulled on her own Earthforms shirt and changed to jeans and put on her sneakers.

When Gabe saw her he said, "Let's get Richard to wear his shirt too. That would be keen-o, as he says."

"Richard already thought of it and I asked him not to."

"Why?"

"I thought it would look silly when we walked in to register me at school."

Kyra came out of the bathroom. "Hey! You're wearing the shirts! I want to take pictures of you all in those shirts. I'll Get Richard's and Demetri's."

When she caught sight of Ben and Zeke, she persuaded

77

them to put on their T-shirts too. Ben's was extra-extra large, and the letters stood out handsomely on his chest.

Kyra didn't believe in lining people up for pictures. "When I take photographs," she had tried to explain to Sara, "I exaggerate the reality. I try to put things together in a way you wouldn't ordinarily look at them. But when I paint, I try to put things together in a way you don't ordinarily see them that will disguise the reality. That's how contradictory I am."

Kyra looked at the group now and ordered them around like a film director. "I want you to climb around the truck. I'm doing black-and-white film, and I can get that shiny metal contrasting with the dark inside the barn." She had Richard park the truck so the name EARTHFORMS lettered on the door would show. "Keep moving. Don't watch me and the camera. Do something. But when I say 'Hold it,' don't move. A bunch of people all labeled Earthforms looks kind of silly climbing over a piece of machinery. Okay — hold it! That's what I want."

Her mention of silliness caught them up, and they formed and reformed groups, like gymnasts building and casting away pyramids.

Sara thought of Richard's expounding last night at supper on his theory that all kinds of art could explode out of a group because one person inspired the next — sometimes in unexpected ways. This kind of happening must be what he was talking about. She grabbed a feather duster that for no sensible reason at all was in the cab of the truck and waved it. Then Ben swung her up on his shoulder, and she held the duster over the back of her head, so it looked like the fancy feathers ladies used to wear to parties. Richard noticed her excitement.

He picked a daisy from a clump by the edge of the ramp and handed it to her with a flourish and a snatch of "You Light Up My Life" sung oratorio-style.

Sara felt lit up. She felt higher than her perch on Ben's shoulder, lighter than the feathers in the duster, brighter than the white of the daisy petals. It was a lovely feeling she wanted to keep. She hoped Richard would stay here forever. With Kyra and Demetri, and Blanche and Harvey, and Ben and Zeke and Gabe. She would tell Gran the next time she wrote that everything was fine. There was a nice woman Richard ought to marry; there was a little boy she'd enjoy as a brother; there were two people who were just like grandparents, even if they could never be blood relations like Gran; there were two nice uncles; and there was a very special boy not much older than she. Richard did seem to be at the center of it all. Surely he'd found his place, and Sara, at last, could share it.

Richard interrupted her thoughts. "To work! We've fooled around long enough. We're off to Martin's Corners to tackle life's earnest needs — grain for the goats and the hens and molasses for Harvey's switchel."

Richard and Gabe crowded her into the cab of the truck between them and Sara's lightheartedness lasted right up to the turnoff to the Northwoods Regional School. Sara asked, "Do we have to go today? It's only the second week in August."

"You might as well get it over and then you won't have to worry about it," Richard advised. "I'll go in to vouch for your vital statistics. Do you know, except for our T-shirts, we don't look related at all? You've got your mother's hair and eyes and somewhere in past generations there must have been a couple of string beans, you're so skinny. Never mind, Sara. You'll fill out. Your mother had a beautiful body."

Sara flushed again. She didn't think her father needed to discuss her looks in front of Gabe, and Richard, intending a compliment, didn't realize he'd trespassed on her sensitivities.

Adding Sara to the school roster was routine. Her transfer records would be requested from Yellow Creek. She would be in the eighth grade of the Northwoods Regional School, to which all the pupils were bused from four country towns. The large building had two wings, one housing the junior high — grades seven through nine — the other housing the high school. A core area contained gyms, cafeteria, auditorium, and offices. After Yellow Creek's modest neighborhood school, the size of the building awed Sara. She was relieved to discover that Gabe would take the same bus and be in the same wing. He'd be in the ninth grade.

In Martin's Corners, Richard parked at the post office. He had a truckful of boxes to mail. "You can meet me here when you've done your errands."

Sara looked at her list. "Blanche wants me to pick up her prescription at the drugstore and get her some thread and some red material. She's promised Demetri she'll make him a Superman cape. Where do I go?"

"I'll show you." Gabe guided her along the main street. In the drugstore, where they waited for Blanche's pills, a blonde girl with blue eyes that seemed as large as yo-yos stepped in front of Gabe. "Hey! Where you been all summer? What's happening?"

"Not much." Gabe waved a hand back and forth between the two girls, as if he were pointing them out to each other. He wasn't practiced at making introductions, but he'd noticed how well Richard's warm manner of calling people's attention to each other worked. "Glenna, this is Sara Bradford. I work for her father. Sara, this is Glenna Johnson. She's a friend of my sister Vonnie. She's in the same class with you."

The girls said "Hi" to each other, but it was obvious to Sara that Glenna wanted Gabe's complete attention. She wasn't at all interested in getting acquainted with another girl. Gabe, however, didn't have much to say about what was or wasn't happening. As soon as Blanche's pills were handed over, he asked, "What's next?"

"Thread and cloth."

Gabe frowned. "I don't know — "

"Try the general store," Glenna said. "There's someone there who's looking for you too — "

"It's probably Vonnie," said Gabe as they crossed the street, "but I don't know why she'd be looking for me." As soon as they stepped into the store he added, "There they are. That's Yvonne with Elise and Annette."

The smallest girl came running to him. He picked her up and hugged her. "Netta! How are you doing?"

"Okay. When are you coming home? Nobody plays Fish with me now."

"Next time I come I'll play ten games with you. Promise!" He kissed her and put her down as his other sisters came over. "Hi, Lise. Hi, Vonnie. This is Sara Bradford."

"Hi." Sara tried a smile and received a scowl and a mutter in return from Vonnie. She saw, though, that Vonnie's unpleasantness was apparently aimed at Gabe.

"Mama told me if I saw you I was to tell you to come home. Papa's been working up to a mean streak because you aren't there to get the stove wood split and stacked, and

Mama's on his ass to get it done. And you lucked out because you're not there to hear them go at each other. Now both of them yell at me. And Mama says don't expect school money or school clothes from them either."

"Tell her I'll buy my own stuff. Mr. Bradford will pay me for the whole summer on Labor Day. And tell her I'm staying on at the barn to work after school and weekends, so I'll earn my own school money. And tell her I'm sorry, but I'm just not coming home to live."

"That don't bother her, that you don't live home," Vonnie said. "What she wants is for you to come home to do some work now and then."

"Let me know when Papa's not around and I'll come split her stove wood."

"That might settle her, but it won't settle Papa. He thinks you ought to give them some money because you're the only one that's been working."

Gabe didn't reply, but it was obvious he didn't agree with his father.

Sara saw that all the girls were dark-haired and dark-eyed like Gabe. Yvonne was stocky and let her hair grow out wildly. Elise and Annette were slender and their faces were pale, yet there was a liveliness about them. None of them paid any attention to Sara, so she looked around for the things Blanche wanted. When she was ready to leave, she found Gabe was not in the store. Yvonne and Elise were handling some fake fur material, and Annette was sitting on the floor, trying to tie a broken shoelace. She was crying.

"Want some help?" Sara asked.

The little girl nodded. Sara put her packages down and took the shoe from Annette. She pulled the lace out and tied a knot in it, rethreaded it, put the shoe on the little girl's foot, and found the lace too short to tie. "You need new laces."

Yvonne turned around. "Stop bawling. If your shoes won't stay on without laces, take the shoes off. We can't buy laces today."

Sara felt in her pocket for some change and held it out to Netta, who reached up for the money.

"Do not accept money from a stranger, Annette." A tall man with abundant white hair and a white mustache stood over the little girl. She pulled her hand back hastily and looked away, avoiding Sara's eyes.

"I'm not a stranger!" Sara protested. "I'm Sara Bradford. I'm a friend of her brother Gabe's."

"A friend of Gabriel Courbeau's?"

"Yes. He works for my father. For Earthforms Pottery."

"I have heard my son is employed there." The man spoke with a slight accent, and he was not at all how Sara expected Gabe's father to be. She had imagined him as a heavy man with a red face, a beer belly, and muscular arms that could land a mean punch. Instead she saw where Gabriel's lean good looks came from, for Mr. Courbeau must have been a handsome man before his dark eyes became red-rimmed and bloodshot and his face deeply creased with a frown. His hands were long-fingered and his body seemed slack. He didn't seem strong enough to strike a boy Gabe's age and inflict much damage until Sara remembered Gabe's saying his father used his belt. As Mr. Courbeau pulled Netta to her feet, Sara glanced at his belt. It had a heavy buckle that was embossed with the design of two crossed rifles. Flailed by an angry man, it would surely leave bruises.

Netta had stopped crying, but she wouldn't look up at

Sara. When Mr. Courbeau said, "Come," she followed him out of the store, stepping carefully to keep her foot from slipping out of the untied shoe. Silently the other two girls followed.

Sara found Gabe waiting around the corner. "I ducked out when I realized Papa had come into the store. What happened?"

Sara told him about Netta's need for shoelaces and Mr. Courbeau's abrupt manner. "I liked your little sister. She must be about Demi's age."

"She's five. I'd bring her over to play with Demi, but my father wouldn't like it. Here's the grocery. What do you need?"

"Molasses. Vinegar." She read down the list Kyra had given her.

She noticed that Gabe had stopped by the notions section and bought two pairs of shoelaces, one red and white, one blue and white. He also bought a package of envelopes, and when they returned to the post office, he put the laces in an envelope, addressed it to Miss Annette Courbeau, and mailed it.

"Netta's the one who gets sent out to the mailbox on the road, and she's always hoped there'll be a letter for her. Usually it's junk mail and bills."

"You like Netta, don't you! A lot of brothers wouldn't bother to send a little sister something in the mail."

"Sure I like little kids. Sometimes I feel sorry for them, like that guy in *Catcher in the Rye* that Richard gave me to read. He felt sorry for little kids. Richard's loaned me a lot of books." If he hadn't been burdened by the bundles they were carrying to the truck, Sara had the feeling he would have flapped his arms around or slapped her on the back to show his enthusiasm. "This has been the best time I've ever had — being at the barn. Getting to read up on all kinds of things. Learning to make pots. Listening to Richard tell about things. He's really fantastic, you know."

"He's fantastic all right. You never can tell what he'll do next." Yet Sara had to admit she'd begun to enjoy her father — to listen for his spontaneous songs of praise and delight, which rose up so often from the pottery — to look forward to being urged to run outside and look at the extraordinary vine with "zillions of cherry tomatoes on it" or to "come out and look at the sky because there's a circus of swallows going on in it" or to "be sure to stop by the pottery and tell me how you like my new teapots and teacups. Should we name them for the Mad Hatter or the Dormouse?" When he couldn't find Gabe or Zeke or Ben for a game of Ping-Pong after supper, she had tried several times to give him a rousing match, and she learned that his shouts of encouragement and threats of revenge were part of his psychological approach to the game — to confuse his opponent into listening to him rather than concentrating on the game. He was also a canny pool player, eager to lure Harvey, who was also skilled, into a match.

At the table it was Richard who made their dinnertimes together so interesting, pulling an anecdote out of Ben and a bit of philosophy out of Harvey; extracting opinions from Blanche and Sara and Gabe and Zeke; asking Kyra to describe a fisherman's boat-blessing on Crete and contrasting it with a festival in Japan; making them all pleased with their contributions to a lively conversation and happy they were sharing it. Sara went to bed at night content with the knowledge that her father was sleeping nearby, letting the world take its course until he was ready to rush out and join it again. She looked back on her sheltered life in Yellow Creek and saw that what she had thought of as secure and reliable was zestless and boring. She knew that being her father at the barn had opened up all kinds of new ideas for her, just as it had for the others.

The only one who didn't seem to be convinced that living and working there was the best possible way of life was Kyra, and the more Sara learned about her, the more she wished that Kyra would be converted. She was good for Richard, Sara was sure. Her common sense made a landing base for his flights of fantasy, and her disposition, balanced between humor and compassion, gave him a sounding board for his tempestuous moods. The warmth and openness Sara discovered in her father now must certainly have developed under Kyra's influence.

At first it had embarrassed Sara when she'd noticed her father resting his hand on Kyra's shoulder or stopping to ruffle her hair and give her a kiss if he hadn't seen her for a few hours. And as for Kyra's demonstrations of affection, that took some getting used to, for Kyra was straightforward and emphatic. When she felt like kissing him she did it energetically, and sometimes it ended up in the kind of kissing Sara had watched on TV close-ups when Gran wasn't around. As if, after tasting each other, they were going to eat each other up, from lips to toes. Sara decided it might be embarrassing to onlookers, but it was reassuring; Kyra and Richard did love each other. *Please let it last,* Sara prayed, hoping that while her prayers were silently made in Esmerelda's benevolent direction, they floated up and beyond to a more omnipotent listener. *Please let Kyra want to stay here with Richard and all of us, and please let her decide to marry him.*

Sara had hoped that the example of Blanche and Harvey, married for fifty years, would influence Kyra and Richard. Then she listened carefully to Blanche and Harvey and wondered how they had stayed married that long. It seemed as if they had nothing in common. Blanche was slow-moving, talkative, and never wanted to be anywhere but in New England, where her people had lived for generations. Harvey was deft, sparing of words, and dreamed of living for a year in Tahiti. "Anyone who has lived through seventy winters in New England deserves at least one year in Tahiti," he claimed. "Now you may think I'm an old man who's kidding himself, but ever since miniature furniture turned into a hot collector's item, I am closer to seeing my dream come true. I can sell every piece I make at a good price. Next spring I'll be ordering the tickets, and the winter after this I'll be under the coconut palms, surrounded by long-haired beauties — and Blanche."

That was a long and fervent speech from Harvey, so fervent that Sara knew his dream must have started in his boyhood and grown over the years. She wondered how he felt when Blanche said, "If you're so set on traveling all that way to sit on a beach, you'd better put the money you've saved in a safer place than where you keep it."

"I don't trust banks."

"You might be sorry. You might end up with about enough money to buy a coconut and take it to Old Orchard Beach, Maine."

"Now, Blanchie, don't worry."

Sara discovered they were always criticizing each other and

telling each other what to do and how to do it. The Wicketts might not be a perfect example of matrimony for Kyra and Richard after all.

Yet on a hot August morning, Sara saw through the talk to the caring. Zeke brought in the latest crop of green beans to freeze, and Blanche prepared to do them.

"I say *do* the beans," she explained to Sara and Demetri who were eating a late breakfast, "because there should be another word than *blanch* for dropping them in hot water and boiling them right through to their little insides."

"Call it what you like, my dear," said Harvey, "but don't tire yourself out. You didn't sleep well last night."

"I'm fine now. Don't fuss."

When Blanche waddled off to the pantry to find some freezer bags, Harvey leaned close to Sara and whispered, "I'd appreciate it if you'd help Blanche. I'm worried about her. She's tried to lose weight all summer and hasn't lost a bit and she's tired but she can't sleep."

"Why doesn't she see a doctor?"

"Because she's stubborn. She won't spend our savings for the trip on having a doctor tell her she's fat. She says she knows that. My Lord! She ought to know I don't care a coconut about Tahiti unless she's there to share it."

"If you told her that, wouldn't she see a doctor?"

"Not Blanchie. She works on opposites. Or on what someone besides me tells her. Maybe I'll ask Richard to talk to her. He's persuasive. Look at how he didn't even know us and in two hours he'd talked us into coming to live here! And he was right. It's the best place we've ever had to live and to work."

Harvey settled Blanche at the table and went off to his shop. Sara sorted and washed beans in the sink. When Demetri asked, "What can I do?" Blanche sent Sara for a yarn needle and string and showed Demetri how to make a necklace out of beans.

Demetri lost interest after he put together necklaces for himself and Sara and Blanche. "Read to me, Sara," he demanded.

"I'm busy. See? I'm filling the sink with cold water and ice cubes to cool the beans."

"I want to sit in the sink and get cool." He climbed onto the countertop and took off his sandals.

"You can't do that," said Blanche, who was chopping the beans with a Chinese cleaver and plunging them into hot water on the stove. "Much as we all love you, Demetri, I don't think we'd appreciate your flavor in the beans. It wouldn't be sanitary to cool the beans with you in the sink."

"But — "

"No buts," said Blanche firmly.

"You go up to my room and choose a book, and as soon as the beans are in the freezer, I'll come and read to you," Sara promised.

She found him lying on her bed, with Fonzie slurped over his shoulder, surrounded by books he'd pulled from her shelves. He chose a story that had goats in it. When Sara finished, her throat was dry. "That's all! My voice is sticking."

Demetri awarded her a sloppy kiss by way of thanks. That gave Sara an idea. Perhaps she could enlist Demetri as a conspirator. "Do you like it here, you and Kyra, living with Richard in the barn?"

"It's some fun. I like Fonzie and Kiddie. I like Richard. I like you. But I miss the beach. The sink isn't big enough to swim — "

"This winter there'll be lots of snow! You can go sledding and make snowmen and you can ski. Skiing is as much fun as swimming. You come whizzing down a mountain and it feels like flying, I guess. I've never tried it but Richard knows how. He can teach us. Won't that be fun? Tell your mother you want to play in the snow and learn how to ski."

"Is it cold? Will I freeze?"

"Your nose and your toes might get cold, but we'd all come home and sit around the stove and get toasty. Kyra and Richard and you and me and Gabe. Wouldn't that be fun?"

"Sure. But if Mama wants to go home and swim, I'd like that better."

"What if Richard and your mother get married? Then Richard will be your father. And this will be your home. Wouldn't you like that?"

"How can Richard be my papa? I already have a papa and I don't want to live with him. I live with my mother, that's who I live with."

Sara could see her idea of forming a conspiracy to urge marriage on Kyra and Richard wouldn't be easy for Demetri to understand. She would have to work on Kyra herself. She would show Kyra how much she needed someone to help take care of Demetri so she could spend more time painting and more time with Richard.

# 7

Sara began a campaign to win Kyra for her father and she needed his cooperation. She suggested that he might like to take Kyra to the movies.

"Do they show movies around here? What do you want to see?"

"Not me. I'll stay home and baby-sit Demetri and you take Kyra. There's a drive-in near Martin's Corners."

"Blanche will baby-sit. I'll take Kyra and you and Gabe. Just find something we'd all enjoy seeing."

"Well," admitted Sara, "that isn't the point."

"What's the point then?"

"You never take Kyra out. All either of you do is work. You're in the pottery or off with Zeke and Gabe at the craft fairs. She's in her studio or off photographing things. You're only together at mealtimes and when you go to bed."

Sara hadn't meant it to sound quite that way. "I mean, you're only together at mealtimes and at night."

"I know what you mean — and you're right. I have been neglecting Kyra. It was different on Crete. There were just the three of us, and now we're part of a group life. People,

people everywhere! You think I should take some special time with Kyra? Has she been complaining?"

"I haven't heard her complain." Sara wished that she had. "But Demi talks about going *home* to Crete to swim and play on the beach. It sounds as if she wasn't sure about staying here through the winter."

"Hmmm, Saradipity, you have made an important point. Much as I shall miss an evening with the assembled company, I should take Kyra out to dine — right?"

"Right."

Later that day Richard saw Sara and reported, rather dramatically, "I have made an assignation. I'm taking Kyra to Boston. And not just to dine. We'll stay overnight at the Copley and we'll spend some time at the art museums and the galleries on Newbury Street. I promised her that you and Blanche could keep Demi healthy and happy. Will you do that?"

"Positively!" Sara was delighted. She hadn't expected one hint to her father to turn into such a venture, or for the two of them, Richard and Kyra, to leave so soon, the very next morning, and in such high spirits.

It was after they left that Sara discovered Blanche was not feeling well enough to get out of bed and that Gabe, who had had a phone call from Vonnie to say his father would be away for the day, had gone home to cope with the woodpile. Zeke and Ben and Harvey were busy in their shops. Sara was on her own with Demetri, and the first thing he asked was, "What can I do?"

Sara thought of the things her mother had taught her to make, that kept her busy when there weren't any other children she could play with. How to fold origami boats and birds.

How to make paper prints. How to make little animals and people out of dough, if she could remember how to make the dough. She suggested to Demetri that they look in the studio for paper and paint. She brought some potatoes, two pie plates, and two vegetable knives. Demetri agreed that making things to surprise Kyra and Richard would be fun. Sara hoped that they would be impressed by the artistic success of their talented offspring and want to encourage it by staying together.

"What do I do?" Demetri looked at a sliced potato-half without enthusiasm.

"Take your knife — carefully, it's sharp — and cut out a shape. Then you stamp the potato in the paint and press it on the paper and it will make a print around your shape. That will be white because you cut it out — so it isn't there to print."

"Huh?" Demetri didn't understand.

"I'll show you." Sara drew a flying bird on the surface and cut it until it dropped out of her potato. Then she found some blue in Kyra's box of acrylic paints, squeezed it onto the pie plate, squizzled the potato around in it, and stamped it onto a piece of newsprint from the big pad Kyra used for quick sketches. There it was — a white sea gull against a patch of blue. She repeated the inking and stamping, overlapping the edges, until she had a flock of gulls flying through a large blue sky.

Demetri was impressed. "I want to make a bird and clouds and a tree and a sunset. I want to print red. I want my own paper."

"Okay. Take a piece off the pad, and I'll find you some red. You cut out the bird and the cloud and the tree — each one on a separate potato." He cut the shapes while Sara hunted through Kyra's paints for red and found a tube that was almost used up. She squeezed it all out on the other pie plate and handed it to Demetri.

"That's not much red," he objected.

"It's all I could find. Where's your paper?"

He grabbed at the pad of newsprint and pulled. The page ripped. "That paper's no good."

"It is thin. There's a big thick piece on that table." It was such a big piece she had to help him lay it flat on the floor. He sat on part of it while he applied his various stamps to the rest. His crude shapes were effective as he scrunched them together, insisting he was printing sunsets. He moved around the paper, sometimes putting the tree in upside down. "I need more red."

"How about yellow? Kyra has a big tube of yellow. If you print it on top of the red, you can put orange into your sunsets."

"I want red, *red*, RED!"

"Okay. There's another box of paints." Sara poked through the tubes. They were small and the colors spilled onto their paper labels, which read "Winsor & Newton," were more subtle. She was particularly taken with the lush rose madder and the brilliant vermillion. "Here — try these." She pressed them out on the plate and Demetri had an orgy of stamping. The different shades of red made splendid hues.

"You can use this too," he said, offering her part of the paper. His knees had picked up the color and they added smudgy prints. Suddenly he dropped his shorts and put as much of his bare bottom into the pie plate as he could. He squidged around and then sat on the paper, rolling about. He was disappointed in the results, as he only left the impression of two circles blending into each other. So he stepped in the paint and added toe blobs to his work. In no time at all, the red paints were used up and Demetri himself looked like a sunset.

"You better wash that off before you bump into any of your mother's paintings!" Sara took him upstairs and ran some water and splashed up some suds in the tub. The red paint floated off him and tinged the soapy foam.

"Ben stepped on my boat." Demetri pointed to a crushed plastic hull. "I want some boats."

Sara wanted to keep him from being noisy so he wouldn't wake up Blanche. "I'll make you some origami boats. Wait while I get some paper." She brought another large sheet from Kyra's studio and cut it into squares. Then she sat on the bathroom floor, carefully folding, creasing, refolding, opening out, and folding back the paper until each piece had turned into a sturdy boat, and a fleet surrounded Demetri. He submerged and rose up with a wave and the boats tumbled about. The paper was tough, so it took him a long time to sink the fleet. When he had accomplished it, Sara and the bathroom were soaked too. "Enough!" she said and pulled the plug. They watched the boats piling up around the drain as the water swirled out, leaving a soggy mess of paper in the tub.

"Now what can I do?" demanded Demetri.

"We could make dough people." Sara thought she remembered now how her mother had mixed the dough. No matter what country they were in, there was always some kind of flour. And water. And sugar or salt. Sara thought it was sugar and that her mother had called it her three-two-one dough. She mixed three portions of one thing to two of another and one of the third. But how much of which? Then she remembered that the dough had sparkled, so she thought it must have had a lot of sugar in it.

In a large bowl she dumped three cups of sugar and two of flour and one of water. "Mix it with your hands, Demi. It will feel like clay and you can make people or turtles or whatever you want."

They mixed, but something was wrong. Instead of a dough, a syrup of goo appeared. "Maybe it was three of flour and two of sugar," Sara said.

"Do it again."

She took another bowl and measured and mixed. This time it was so stiff she had to add more water. When it was right, they worked away. Demetri made his turtles. He made rocks for them to sit on. He made fish for them to catch. He tried to make a dog. "What are you making?"

"This is a castle. I'm putting a rope ladder down from the tower window."

"Why?"

"So the princess can come and go when she wants without anyone checking up on her."

"Why?"

"Because she likes to have secrets."

"Why?"

"Demi! How do I know. She just does."

"I want to do something else now." He swept his arm out and hit the bowl full of the syrupy mix. It broke, sending the goo cascading over the table, the chair, and the floor. It splashed onto Fonzie and matted his fur. He protested with a yowl and began licking it off.

Sara picked up the broken crockery and dropped it in the trash, hoping it wasn't something special that Richard had made. She mopped up the table and made a swipe at the chair seats.

"Wipe up the puddle on the floor." Sara handed Demetri a batch of paper towels. "Then we'll put our dough things in the oven to bake."

She had learned from Blanche how to make a fire in the stove and arrange the dampers so it would muddle along. Then she found two roasting pans and put his figures in one and her castle in the other and loaded them into the oven. "Just like cooking pots in Richard's kiln. Only it doesn't take as long."

"How long?"

"About an hour." She washed the remaining bowl in the sink. She felt competent as a baby sitter and an artist and a cook. Using the oven inspired her. "How about picking blueberries? The oven will be warm from cooking the dough things, and I could bake a cake or a pie." Sara had never made a cake or a pie, but she was willing to try.

"Okay." Demetri liked to eat berries off the bush.

Sara left a note on the kitchen table. "Demi and I are picking berries. Back in an hour." She noticed it was only eleven o'clock, but she felt as if she and Demetri had spent days in each other's company.

They left the barn, passing under the tree with the swinging rope and taking the path up the hill. Gabe had tethered the goats, and they gave a few bleats, twitched their ears, and shook their bells as Sara and Demetri passed by. Sara saw that Fonzie had followed partway up the hill, but he was afraid of the goats. She saw him lie down, an orange cat in a tigerish pose in a patch of sun that overlaid the grass, intensifying its green into an emerald brilliance. It was like looking at a cat in a painting, a cat she didn't know — something familiar suddenly seen in a new way. The kind of thing Kyra talked about doing in her work.

"Come on!" Demetri ran into the woods, and she hurried to catch up with him. The path was plain to see, and there was the great boulder for a landmark. Sara turned toward the swamp, walking into the underbrush. Demetri pretended he was a hunter. "Be quiet!" he ordered. "You'll frighten the lions."

She was surprised when they reached the place where the high bush berries were that only a few remained on each bush. Between hungry birds and the hot weather of the last week, the great crop had dwindled. The ones that were left were so dry and puckered they weren't worth picking. "We'll have to look farther," Sara told Demetri. She eased into the scratchy underbrush.

"I'm an explorer!" Demetri announced. He followed her happily until a branch she let go too quickly hit him like a whip in the face. He screamed.

"I'm sorry!" Sara was distressed to see the red welt appearing on his cheek and tried to comfort him. "You go first. You be the chief explorer."

The bushes were thick and most of them were taller than his head, and it was a disappointing expedition. There didn't seem to be a bush with blueberries anywhere.

"I want to go home." Demetri sat down under an arching hobblebush.

So did Sara. She wished she knew what direction home was in. She looked up, wishing for a sign from the sky — even a cloud going in a particular direction. She saw only blank blue space.

"You're lost," Demetri accused her.

"No, I'm not. The woods around here aren't big enough to be lost in. Come on."

"Carry me."

"You're big enough to carry me!"

"I'll stay here. I'll be all lonely. I'll die. You'll be sorry."

Sara squatted beside him. The bush arched over her, and as she crouched there, she remembered a time when she had felt so lonely she was sure she would die — all alone — and Richard and her mother would be sorry. They were in Italy; the kitchen floor was stone and it was cold, and she must have been even younger than Demetri because she couldn't tie her shoelaces. She'd kept tripping on them, so she'd taken her shoes off. She'd been as despairing as Annette had been, sitting on the floor of the general store with her broken lace.

Sara remembered, too, that her knee socks were old and wouldn't stay up, so she'd taken those off. She couldn't button her blouse and her skirt. She'd called and called but no one had heard her. No one had come. She had been so frightened that she had hidden under a table covered by a cloth that hung almost to the floor. Perhaps it was sitting under a bush that awakened the memory. She had sat there on the cold stone in her underpants and her shivering skin for a long time. A woman dressed in black had shuffled in. She wore felt slippers and Sara had thought how warm her feet must be. She had gone into the bedroom where Sara slept, and when she didn't see her, came running back, calling out something about the bambina, the bambina — and Sara hadn't said a word. It could have been minutes later or hours later when her father returned. He had rushed her mother, who had appendicitis, to a hospital and asked the lady who ran the pensione to look after Sara. When he'd come back, the lady said she couldn't find Sara. The *bambina* had gone. What laments! What noise! What rushings about — and finally Sara had cried out and her father had found her under the table. He'd hauled her out and scolded in what seemed to her terrifying tones, although he had promised never to leave her alone again. So much for promises, Sara thought.

"I'll carry you a little," she said to Demetri, because she had remembered how terrible it was to be small and afraid. "Just till we come to a path." She tried to perch him on her hip, as Kyra did so easily, but she was thin and he kept slipping. He had to clutch her tightly around the neck.

Five minutes later she was breathing hard, and Demetri's weight grew heavier with each step. She was about to put him down so she could rest, when she stepped onto a path.

"See — there's a path. We'll go downhill. It's easier." Soon the way widened and suddenly it stopped at the top of a gravel bank, where stone and soil had been taken away and the remaining hollow was filled with trash. Looking ahead, Sara saw the gleam of a tin roof among the trees. "There's a house. Now we can find out where we are."

They slid down the steep bank, Sara putting out a hand to keep Demetri from falling. Then he stumbled and fell beyond her, rolling faster and faster. At the bottom his head struck a sharp-edged rock with a nasty thwack. This time it was Sara who screamed, because he didn't move.

A dog barked, a familiar, rumbling series of woofs, and Sara called. The dog came running and, as she hoped, it was Mickey. They were near the Courbeau place.

Demetri sat up. A gash under one eye spewed blood down his cheek and a lump rounded up under the skin on his forehead. As he already had a welt on his other cheek, he looked badly wounded. Sara picked him up and walked as fast as she could toward the house. Demetri sobbed, but he seemed quite limp and made no effort to clutch her as he had before. Sara heard someone chopping wood. "Gabe! Come help!"

Gabe was surprised to see her. He dropped his ax and hurried to lift the little boy out of her arms. "I'll take him into the house. You better come too. Just don't expect my mother to help."

Sara noticed that the house was tall, topped by a tin roof, some parts of it new and shiny, some old and red-brown with rust. They passed a barn, which looked as if it tilted one more inch it would fall over. Two trucks rested in various states of decay. Old tires, wooden crates, broken farm implements lay about. Hens and ducks stalked away, clucking in annoyance at the sudden commotion.

Sara sensed that Gabe, although he was worried by Demetri's wounds, wasn't pleased at having to take her into his house. They crossed the back porch, which held a washing machine, a wringer, a wooden icebox with half its doors off, and a playpen. A fat two-year-old in bulging plastic diapers held up his arms and screeched.

"Pee-you!" said Gabe as he walked by. "Not now, Francie. I'm busy." Francie put his thumb in his mouth and held onto the pen with his other hand, rocking back and forth, making the rickety pen squeak. But when they went into the kitchen and the door slammed behind them, Francie took his thumb out and screeched again.

Gabe set Demetri on a table crowded with boxes of cereal and crackers and bottles of ketchup and instant coffee. Demetri sat up without help, but he kept shrieking.

"Got any ice, Mama?" Gabe called.

"In the trays." A woman wearing a quilted bathrobe so worn that the batting showed through in spots appeared in the doorway. She was small, gray-haired, and, Sara knew from her protuberant shape, pregnant. She didn't offer to help. "Give Francie a doughnut when you go out. He's hungry."

"He's got a load in his pants. Where's Vonnie or Elise? I can't take care of him now."

"Eee–vonne!" Mrs. Courbeau had a loud voice. "Eeeee-vonne! Get out here." Then, as if she suddenly realized she was the lady of the house, she looked at Sara and said, "How do you do." Without waiting for an answer, she went back into the other room, out of Sara's sight.

Gabe pulled an ice tray out of the refrigerator and banged it on the table. "Hand me a towel, Sara. There's one near the sink."

She found a fairly clean dish towel. Gabe put the ice in it and held it to Demetri's cut. "You're all right, Demi. It's not as bad as you think. If you can yell that loud, your head's going to be fine."

Another door opened and Yvonne walked in. "You can't even have a quiet day when the old man's not here. What's with Francie?"

"He needs changing. I'm busy."

Sara saw Yvonne aim a disgusted look toward the room where her mother was watching a TV soap opera whose dialogue she had turned up loud enough to hear over the crying children. Yvonne opened a drawer, took out a diaper, and went to cope with her brother. Gabe held the ice away from Demetri's cheek. They could see how jagged and dirty the cut was.

"He ought to have stitches," Gabe said. "You'd better phone Richard."

"He's in Boston with Kyra."

"Then see if Ben's there. The phone's on the wall."

She let the phone ring and ring until Ben answered. She explained.

"We wondered why you hadn't come back, especially when you left whatever those things are to burn up in the oven. I'll come and take Demi to the clinic."

"Thank you." Sara sat down at the table, suddenly aware of being hot, tired, dried out with thirst, and depressed over all the things that had gone wrong with her good intentions: Demetri hurt and the beautiful dough creations turned, according to Ben, into stinking cinders. "Could I have a cold drink?"

"Sure." Gabe found a can of Tab for her. Yvonne came back, walked past without saying a word, went into her room, and shut the door. Annette and Elise came into the kitchen because the visitors were more interesting than the soap opera.

"I've had stitches." Elise showed Sara a long scar on her shin.

"I want stitches," said Annette. "I'll go get some too."

"You don't want stitches, Netta," Gabe told her. "Not on your face like Demetri."

"Will I get a scar?" Demetri, aware that all eyes were on him, stopped crying. "Will I look like a pirate?"

"Probably," Gabe said.

Demetri hiccupped with a satisfied sob, wiggled off the table and onto Sara's lap. He rested his head on her shoulder, and Sara felt he'd renewed his trust in her. Everything would be all right.

## 8

Sara planned to tell Richard and Kyra, when they returned the next evening, all the things she had done to keep Demetri happy. She would show them the printed sunsets and tell them about the dough figures even though she'd had to throw them away. Blanche, who came downstairs when Ben brought Sara and Demetri home, refused to let her keep one cindery lump. "They smell and they shed black crumbs."

"We can make some more," Demetri suggested.

"Not tonight. It will take a lot of cleaning up — you made such a mess."

Sara thought Blanche was being unfair, because she and Demetri had made an attempt to get rid of the mess.

"Did you make glue too?" Zeke asked. "I got up from the table at lunch and the chair came with me. Stuck to my pants!"

Demetri giggled. Sara gave him a warning look. She didn't want to discuss her syrupy mistake any more than her leaving the things to overcook in the oven.

"And what about all that pulp paper in the tub?" asked Harvey. "You running a paper mill up there?"

"Where did you find that paper?" Zeke asked. "It doesn't feel like your everyday sleazy paper products."

"From Kyra's studio."

"Big sheets?"

"Yes. Why?"

"I hope it wasn't the special watercolor paper she was telling me about that's so expensive. Ben, how about going to Portsmouth with me tomorrow afternoon? It might be a good time to be away from it all."

Zeke was joking, but Ben seemed concerned. Perhaps he was remembering his talk with Sara in his shop the day she arrived, after Fonzie had leaped into the punch bowl and Richard had exploded in wrath.

"Look, Sara, Demetri hasn't been badly hurt," Ben said. "Whatever mistakes you've made aren't fatal. Get a good night's sleep and don't worry. Richard and Kyra will have had such a good time they won't be too upset."

Sara hoped he was right; but she spent an uneasy night and a long day, waiting for judgment. Even usually comforting Blanche seemed put out with her; she spent her time upstairs, crocheting, and said she was too tired from cleaning up after Sara to play cribbage. Even worse, Demetri ran a fever and lay on Blanche's bed, complaining that his face hurt. Blanche called the clinic and the doctor prescribed penicillin. Harvey had to make a trip for the medicine, because Ben and Zeke had gone off to Portsmouth. They said if Kyra and Richard could take a vacation, they could too, and a seafood dinner would be a good change from farm food. They'd taken Gabe with them because he seemed so down after his day at home.

Richard and Kyra took their time about returning from the city, and Sara was reading in bed when she heard the truck crunch over the gravel below her window. She could pretend to be asleep and hope by morning her deeds wouldn't seem so dreadful, yet she didn't want Kyra to discover Demetri without being warned about the odd pattern of bristly black stitches sprouting out of his cheek and the other lumps and bumps on his face. In her bathrobe and slippers, she went down to the kitchen and found Kyra and her father drinking tea.

"Saradipity!" Her father swept her into a hug. "I told Kyra you are the one to thank for our little vacation. We had the greatest time!"

"It was wonderful," Kyra agreed. "Thanks, Sara. *Real* thanks."

"It wasn't so great here and everything is my fault and I want to tell you about it right now."

"Then sit down," said Richard, who seemed amused by her seriousness, "and confess. I will be calm."

Sara didn't want him to tease about being calm. She hoped he meant it. "I took Demi to pick berries and he fell down a gravel bank and hit his face and Ben took him to the clinic and he has seven stitches and he ran a fever but Blanche phoned the doctor and Harvey got some penicillin and the doctor said Demetri will be all right. Except he'll have a scar."

"Great going, Sara!" Richard said. "A nonstop sentence!"

"Don't, Richard," said Kyra. She put her arms around Sara. "Thank you for telling me before I went upstairs and discovered it. Why do you think Demetri's taking a tumble and cutting his face was your fault?"

"Because I took him off in the woods."

"He could have tripped and fallen off the ramp right here. You can't blame yourself for an accident like that."

"But that's not all of it."

"Good Lord!" exclaimed her father. "Fonzie attacked the pots again."

"No." Sara turned white.

"Really, Richard!" said Kyra. "You're frightening her."

"Never! Am I frightening you, Sara?"

Sara could hear Gran saying, "Stand up to your father." She tried. She said, "You're not making it easy. You're needling me and putting me down."

Richard, who obviously felt he had been exhibiting not only calm but humor, looked hurt. "I'm sorry you see it that way."

Kyra said, "Give Sara a chance now. So what else happened?"

"I was trying to do things with Demi to keep him busy because Blanche stayed in bed yesterday. So I took some paper and paints from your studio, and Zeke told me that the paper we used was very expensive."

"The huge sheets of heavy paper I left on the table? There were two of them."

"That's where we found them. Demi printed red sunsets on one. With a potato. He sat in the paint and printed himself too. It came out quite interesting. You might even like it." Sara searched Kyra's face, hoping to see a gleam of amusement or a spark of artistic interest or even motherly pride in a son's accomplishment.

"Where did you find the paint?"

"In your boxes. There was some rose stuff and some vermillion."

"The vermillion! All used up?"

Sara nodded.

"My treasured vermillion! My expensive d'Arches hand-made paper!" Kyra sounded mournful.

"That was damn thoughtless, Sara." Richard glared at her. "You should never use anything of anybody's without permission. And to use an artist's expensive materials that way is inexcusable."

"Maybe I can salvage some of it. Did you make prints on both sheets?" Kyra asked. "Maybe I can paint on the other side."

"It's worse. I cut the other one up into smaller pieces. To make boats for Demi when I put him in the tub to wash off the paint." Sara broke into guilty sobs at the same time Kyra broke into ripples of laughter.

Richard stared at both of them. "What's the tremendous tragedy?" he asked Sara. "What's so damn funny?" he asked Kyra.

"I can hardly wait to see the flaming sunsets. And the dreadfully expensive paper boats."

"I undid them." Sara wept. "The pieces are drying out flat. I'll save up to buy you some more paper."

"Oh, Sara! Do stop crying!" Kyra exclaimed. "The world won't end if I don't do those paintings now. After all, I owe you something for baby-sitting. I didn't realize Blanche was down with a bad spell. I'd say we were even."

Richard mischievously sang a snatch from *The Mikado* about the punishment fitting the crime. Kyra shushed him. "Actually there are two good things. Demi didn't have a concussion and neither of you got paint in your mouths. Vermillion used to be made from cinnabar. Doesn't that sound romantic? Now it's made from sulphur and mercury. Toxic as can be. Anyway, I'm grateful to you for persuading Richard that we needed a break away from the farm. So go back to bed, Sara, and have a good night's sleep. I'm not really cross with you and I do love you."

Sara stood still, surprised, and then alight with hope. She'd heard Gran part with those words "I love you" on rare occasions, as if she only had a few of them to use and had to save them up rather than spend them. Kyra loved Richard, and if she loved Sara too, perhaps she would stay and perhaps she would marry her father.

Sara hugged the words inside her, and even when she saw how absorbed Kyra was by her work during the next days, she felt she was now part of Kyra's life too. She was encouraged enough to turn to her for advice after she had spent a frustrating Labor Day morning facing facts. Gran had made her dresses for muggy southern weather. New Hampshire would soon offer crisp mornings edged with snappy winds. After lunch she asked Kyra to look at her clothes for school. The meager collection was spread out on her bed. "What can I wear the first day of school? That's two days from now. One pair of my jeans is all paint y and the other is too patchy."

"What do the girls wear here? Jeans? Dresses?"

"I'll ask Gabe. I hope it's not dresses. Mine are too short, too old, and too thin. I'd freeze in them."

Kyra picked up the pastel cottons. "These are horrible! Why didn't you yelp sooner? I'm not good at creating something out of a curtain, like Scarlett O'Hara."

"I didn't want to think about school."

"I'll take you to Manchester to shop tomorrow — if Richard will give you some money."

Sara looked for Gabe first. She found him stretched out on the deck, wearing cut-offs and inviting a last layer of summer sun. For a moment she didn't disturb him; she admired his supple body, the soft curve of his lips, and the sweep of his dark lashes. She seldom saw him doing nothing, and even now his hands didn't look relaxed. As she stared at him, she was surprised at the tingling sensation that rushed through her and embarrassed when he became aware of her and sat up.

"Want to join me getting a last-minute tan?" he asked.

"I'd only freckle and frizzle." Sara's fair skin annoyed her, as it never tanned evenly. She knew, though, that her reddish-gold hair looked good after Kyra had trimmed and shaped it for her several times during the hot weather. "What do the girls wear to school here?"

"How do you mean? They look good, but I don't think they get dressy. My sisters don't. But then they have to play Pass. Vonnie hands on stuff to Lise and Lise passes stuff to Netta."

"I mean, do they wear jeans and sweaters, or skirts and tops, or dresses?"

"All of the above. Then when it gets cold everyone wears pants and shirts and vests and boots and parkas. Good, warm, windproof stuff. I'm going to buy boots and a new parka. Richard paid me this morning for three months' work."

"Would you like to shop in Manchester tomorrow with Kyra and me?"

"Sure. Martin's Corners doesn't have a good boot place."

Sara found Kyra in the studio and gave her report. "I need sweaters and skirts and pants. And boots and a parka. Can Gabe go with us? He needs things too."

"Sure, and I'll take Demi. We could use warm clothes too. I'll splurge a little because I may sell a painting. I left two on consignment in a gallery in Boston."

"How's it going?" Sara felt close enough now to Kyra to ask.

"I've been doing new things." Kyra's eyes gleamed with confidence. "I found ways to work out the problems in those paintings that were baffling me." She waved a hand toward unframed canvases and watercolors taped to panels that leaned against the wall.

Sara saw that they shimmered with tones and shadows that insinuated themselves into all kinds of surprises. She thought they looked like shapes held in suspension until they decided to change of themselves. "What do you call that kind of painting?"

"Organic, maybe?" Kyra shrugged. "It seems to have evolved out of my painting-what-I-must-say period. Call it anything you like." She gave Sara a generous hug. "It feels so great to be in control of my work again. When I go back to Crete, I can try doing my old subjects this way."

"Go back to Crete?" Sara was alarmed.

"Eventually. I have to. I own a house there and I promised Demi's father he could have access to him at least half of each year. I don't want Georgios jetting over here to see him, that's for sure!"

"It wouldn't be easy when you're with Richard. Couldn't you just take Demi to Greece for a quick visit and come back?"

"You really want me to stay here, don't you?"

"I want you to marry Richard."

There. It was out. No more secret dreaming and hoping.

Kyra, dressed vividly in her scarlet T-shirt and once-white carpenter's overalls that were now as stained as her paint rags, sat on a stool, and the strong light from the north window intensified the strength of her pose: the firm way she carried her head, the straightness of her back, the purpose in her look.

Sara could almost feel the connection existing between Kyra's observant eye and her skilled hand. She felt those observing eyes now considering her soberly.

"So I have to convince you as well as Richard that I'm not good at family life. At being a wife and a mother — "

"Demi — " began Sara.

"I'm finding my way with him," Kyra interrupted. "I can't handle more than that now. Demetri and my painting are all. Much as I love your charming and occasionally difficult father — and much as I love you, Sara — I can't take you both on. Love is important, and I am more than grateful for Richard's love and for yours. But it takes commitment to put together a family and keep it together. I failed at that once. And for now my commitment is to myself. And to Demi. Just as yours, Sara, must be to yourself. And to Richard, if you can be grown up and understanding enough."

Kyra saw the tears that Sara's dashed dreams caused and reached out to pull her close. "Try to understand. There are times when we need all the family love and support we can have and we can be absolutely selfish about it. After Georgios and I broke up, I spent weeks at home with my parents until I knew I couldn't be their child anymore. It's been harder for you. You don't feel much like anyone's child, do you?"

"Not since my mother died."

"So what do you want, Sara? No one can replace your own mother, you know. Certainly not me!"

"I know that, but I'd like someone to be like a mother to me. Just for a little while. And I guess I'd really like a father who wanted to be called Father or Daddy. Richard seems to want to be more like a friend than a father."

Kyra held Sara close and patted her back, as if she were

Demetri's age. It was what Sara needed and wanted, and she could have gone on resting in Kyra's arms for a long time. But after a bit Kyra pulled away. "You might like having a mother for a few months, but then you'd be at the age where most girls start to disagree with their parents and rebel against them. You've almost made it there on your own. You'll be grown up and independent ahead of the others, and you won't have to untie apron strings the way most kids do."

"You think I'm silly to think I'm missing something?"

"No. It's just that I can't be your missing mother. And it's not realistic to expect Richard to suddenly want to be called Daddy when he never really seems to have accepted the role."

"Maybe not." Sara went on to something else that bothered her. "He acts kind of fatherly to Demetri."

"Oh, he's great at hugging and loving Demetri. But he's not great at backing me up when I have to discipline him. Somehow Richard has always disappeared when I've had to make Demi behave." Kyra handed Sara a Kleenex. "We both have problems with our men, don't we! Now — do make a list of what you need for school and ask Richard for the money. We'll go off tomorrow and make a day of it."

Sara went looking for Richard. "He's taking a shower," Demetri told her. Richard had showered and gone elsewhere. "Probably not to the pottery," Blanche guessed. "I think he's taking an afternoon off. He's finally realized it's a holiday." Blanche sat on her chaise, crocheting an afghan in orlon of the violent colors that her father swore only the colorblind would buy. Yet Sara knew that each time Harvey took one along to a craft fair, someone always bought it.

Blanche asked, "What are you up to?"

Sara had discovered that Blanche's annoyance with her

when Demetri was hurt had been temporary, the result of her not being well herself. Their friendship and their cribbage games had been resumed with eagerness on both sides. "Making a shopping list for school clothes. What you wear the first day at a new school is important."

"Of course! You must walk in like a princess. Pull my magic chest over here, and I'll find something for you that's worthy of the occasion." Blanche swung her legs over the edge of the chaise and sat up. Sara started to tell her that she knew what she wanted to buy, but she could see Blanche needed to offer something.

When the chest was opened, Sara looked on the contents with awe and dread. There were silk blouses edged with tatting in brilliant colors and crepe evening dresses with imitation pearls sewed on in whirly patterns. Sequins flashed on tie-dyed chiffon, and scarlet satin rippled as Blanche held it up to admire. How could Sara turn down Blanche's offerings without hurting her feelings?

"I remember my favorite outfit when I was a senior in high school," Blanche told her. "It was what we called a twin set. A cardigan over a matching short-sleeved sweater. It was angora and such a beautiful purple color. Harvey loved it, even when it shed all over him."

Sara knew that Blanche and Harvey had gone together all through school and married right after high school graduation. Blanche sighed and put down the red satin. "I guess these are all party clothes."

Sara was relieved. "I'll know where to come when I want to dress up."

She discovered Richard pursuing a game of Ping-Pong with Zeke and waited until he'd won a hard-fought point. "Could you give me some money so I can shop for school clothes to-morrow with Kyra?"

"How much do you need?"

Sara tried to add up boots, pants, parka, turtlenecks, slacks, a skirt, some sweaters, and knee socks in her head. "Maybe a hundred and fifty dollars."

"Oof!" Richard frowned. "You've caught me short. I paid Gabe his share for the summer's work and paid the electricity bill, which is stupendous with all the machinery clonking away, and I'm temporarily broke. We have good production and good prospects, but poor cash flow at the moment."

Harvey looked up from the *Country Journal* he was reading. "Richard, speaking as a member of this group, I say that's not true. You don't have cash because you're underwriting all the basic bills. But I have cash and I'd be delighted to give — "

"Thanks, Harvey, but — "

"Call it a rent payment then. You're no businessman! Ben and I've been talking and we want to pay you for our work-space and the electricity we use. It's past due. Actually, if you rented out the rest of the space on the second floor, you could make money on the barn."

Richard looked surprised at that thought.

Harvey stood up. "Sara, come along and let me give you some cash, and then Ben and I will sit down with your im-practical father and put this on a sensible basis."

Harvey led her to his shop. He took a key from his wallet and opened a roll-top chest on his work table. "This was my grandfather's desk. He was a sea captain." When Harvey pulled out a drawer, the roll-top section slipped back out of the way, revealing a set of pigeonholes, and each of the pigeon-holes was filled with green-and-white bundles. Harvey took out a bundle and Sara saw it was a roll of bills. He pulled off a hundred-dollar bill and a fifty and handed them to her. "I don't believe in banks, not after my father lost all his savings when his bank failed in the Depression. I never used to have enough money to worry about where I kept it and I'm not going to worry now. This will all go on a deposit with a travel agent anyway. There — that's toward what I owe Richard and — " he added three tens — here's a present from Blanche and me. Buy something pretty like a blouse with roses on it. Blanche always looked swell in roses. And you're just as pretty as Blanche was at your age."

"Thanks, Harvey. Thanks a lot!" Sara kissed his wrinkly cheek. As she returned to the common room, Gabe was looking for her. "You've got to hear this! It's a record of whales — singing."

"You're kidding!" Sara's curiosity was netted. She went to sit on cushions on the floor with Richard and Kyra and Zeke and Gabe and listen.

She found that the eerie echoing sounds of the whales made her sad. There was something spine-shivering about their messages, and she wondered if it was because each of them was alone in a depth of blackness, as anxious to be heard and understood as she was, and afraid that no one would hear, or no one could understand. She heard their songs as lonely cries for help.

Her father, however, heard them differently. "They are making miracles of music. Mindful music. That's what I should have done with my life!" he announced dramatically. "Been a zoologist or a mammalogist — or whatever you call people who specialize in studying the mysteries of the great whales. Helped to save them. Done something humanly significant. More vital than ceramics." Then, with an enormous sigh, he admitted, "It's too late now. My best years have gone into dishes."

Sara saw that Gabe was startled by her father's announcement and seemed worried until Richard settled back and let the look of frantic disappointment fall from his face. Sara would have been upset too, except that she had discovered that her father often made sudden statements of self-analysis. Like his announcing several days ago his conviction that he should have been a brain surgeon. And later saying he should have been a statesman — instead of devoting his life to inanimate objects. Now she just took the remarks for what they were worth: wishful thinking. The same kind of wishful thinking that she'd exposed to Kyra and that, barring a miracle, would not come true.

# 9

"How did the first day at school go?" Blanche asked Sara at the supper table.

"It wasn't bad," Sara reported. "I have a Mr. Worthington for home room. It's his first year teaching and he does social studies. There's a girl who's in most of my classes — Margaret Allen. I like her and she introduced me to some kids. One's named Cherylene Benedetto, who says to call her Cherylene. No nickname. She was sorry for me because she said Sara is such a plain name."

"Tell her it's short for Saradipity." Richard grinned at her.

"Why do you call me that sometimes? I always wondered."

"I wanted to name you Serendipity, but your mother insisted on Sara. Serendipity, you know, means something happy that you discover accidentally, unexpectedly."

"So you weren't planning to have kids and you didn't expect me?"

"Hardly. We knew for months you were coming." Richard was being a stickler for physiology and semantics.

That annoyed Sara. "But I was an accident." She made it a statement, not a question.

"I told you — you were serendipitous. And this public

118

forum, Sara, is not the place to discuss personal matters." Her father tried a humorous quirk to his voice, but Sara saw he really didn't like the subject she'd brought up. He was trying to pass it off as her bad manners.

"Isn't being a father rather personal!" The words erupted before Sara could stop them.

A gap of silence followed her outburst. When it was obvious that Richard wasn't going to reply, when he made a business out of passing the green beans and asking for the salad, everyone talked at once. Sara felt Richard had let her down yet again.

Blanche rattled on about names. "I wish you could choose your own name. I never would pick Blanche. It's so washed out. Maybe that's why I love to surround myself with beautiful colors."

Ben asked, "Do you know why your mother wanted to name you Sara?"

"It was her mother's name — my Gran's name. She's Sara Evalina Kincaid." It was odd to think of wrinkled Gran as Sara Evalina, and what she might have looked like when she was a girl. At thirteen, for instance — Sara's age. It was odd too that until Ben's question she hadn't realized some of the implications of being named for her grandmother. Perhaps it had been a link her mother needed to remind her of home and family. Perhaps it was another source of the guilty feelings that kept her father from being close to her. It reminded him of Gran's disapproval of his wanderings and her blaming him for her daughter's death far away from home.

In his quiet manner Ben went on drawing out some of Sara's hurt. "Do you think my name is short for Benjamin?"

"Isn't it?"

"No. It's just Ben. A small name for a big man, eh! Names don't mean much unless you make something of them. Like the Franklin stove is named for Ben Franklin. I like to think that maybe a hundred years from now my tables will be called Tillsit tables, and I wonder if they will mean as much to the people who use them as they did to me when I was making them." Suddenly he stopped, aware that others besides Sara were listening to him, and he hastily asked Zeke to pass him the potatoes. "These potatoes taste great. They only need a bit of butter and a smidge of salt."

"Speaking about names — or words," said Richard, eager for a conversation he felt comfortable with, "that's a funny one. Smidge. Smidgeon. What do you think that means, Sara?"

She shrugged. She didn't care. She wanted to listen to Ben talk about how he thought about things.

"It means a very small quantity. A smitch. And that goes back to a smutch, which means a smudge or a stain. Fascinating. I think we should play Dictionary. Best game I know to tune up the mind. Gabe, please fetch a dictionary and paper and pencils."

Zeke excused himself. "Brain games aren't my thing, folks. I'd rather go carve some wood."

"Me too," said Harvey. "I'm making a Winthrop desk with a secret drawer. Now that tunes up the hand — making a miniature desk with a miniature secret drawer."

"Insubordination! Rank desertion!" Richard pretended to bluster. "Go your untutored ways."

Gabe brought a dictionary and paper and pencils.

"I'm going to find a word in the dictionary and tell it to you," Richard announced. "If none of you knows what it means, that's the word each of us will write down. Then you each make up a definition for it. It can be funny or sneaky or formal, like a dictionary definition. And I write down the real definition and shuffle it in with the others. When I read them all out loud, you vote on which is the real definition. Anyone who guesses right gets a point. Anyone whose wrong definition gets votes gets a point for each vote. All clear?"

"I can't read that book," Demetri complained, "and I print slow."

"You take your turn with me," said Richard. "Sit on my lap and open the dictionary and shut your eyes and point to a word, and we'll see if anyone knows it."

Demetri made a great show of flapping the pages open and stabbing a word with his finger. "What's it say?"

"It says *melisma*. M–E–L–I–S–M–A. Anybody know what it means? No? Okay, write it down and make up something. That's a good one, Demi."

Sara wrote down *melisma* and couldn't think of what to write next. She watched Gabe, heard him say, "Hey!" and grin over the definition he'd made up. Blanche looked puzzled, Kyra had a secret smirk, and Ben frowned. Eventually they all wrote something.

"Ready, Sara?" Richard asked. "Or still thinking?"

Sara stared at *melisma*. It sounded swampy and sad. She wrote: *melisma: a state of being sad. Feeling funky.*

Richard unfolded all the papers and read the definitions aloud with glee. When he came to Sara's he said it carefully. "A state of being sad. Someone's tuning up his mind."

*His* mind, noted Sara. He probably thinks Gabe or Ben wrote it.

When he read the definitions over again, pausing to count

any votes each received, Kyra and Gabe voted for hers. That surprised her, but she tried not to let it show. She forgot to vote until Richard said, "Last one. *Melisma — a passage sung to one syllable of text*, as in Gregorian chant. Who votes for that?"

"I do," said Sara.

"Well–well–well — " Richard looked at her in surprise. "You hit it. That's what *melisma* means. And you fooled two people, so you get two points for your melancholy state of mind. Well done, Sara — old girl!"

She wondered if he had started to call her Saradipity and thought better of it. But she liked the game. She wanted to play it again, and it became an after-supper tradition.

Soon the September days fell into a pattern too. She and Gabe were out on the roadside waiting for the school bus by seven o'clock. Kyra and Richard were not early risers, and in that casual household no one had an alarm clock. "I'm against them," Richard protested when Sara suggested she and Gabe needed one so they wouldn't miss the bus. "No one should be jolted into awareness by the shrilling of a loud uncontradictable mechanism. It's inhuman."

"How about me for an alarm clock?" Ben suggested. "I wake up at six from sheer habit. I'll get Gabe up and I'll knock at your door, Sara."

Which he kindly did every morning. Then, if he didn't hear a reply from her, he opened her door and said in a gruff voice, "Sara Bradford, hop out of bed or I'll send the trolls after you." That made Sara laugh because he was reversing Harvey's line with Demetri about hopping into bed before the trolls got him. Sometimes Sara didn't answer so she could hear Ben say it.

Gabe didn't talk in the morning. He cooked his eggs and made his toast and drank his coffee, and if Sara was dawdling he was apt to say, "See you — " and start for the bus without her. At first she was puzzled by his not waiting for her; then she realized he probably wouldn't have waited for his sisters either. So she tried hard to be ready when he was.

The bus was usually half full when it stopped for them, and often he slid into a seat next to a friend from his grade. Before long Sara found friends to sit beside. One was Rob Luther, who was in her social studies class, and he was usually doing his soc homework on the bus. He claimed that Worthington was only about two pages ahead of them, reading their text for the first time, so he wasn't going to break his brains for that class.

Yvonne boarded the bus at the next stop, but she didn't attempt to sit with her brother. She barely talked to him and she never said more than "Hi" to Sara.

Occasionally Richard asked, "Do you like it at Northwoods? Are you getting along all right?" Sara didn't have any choice, apparently, of going anywhere else, but he did seem interested. "What class do you like best?"

Sara wasn't sure. She liked the English teacher and the art class was fun, but any form of math was torture. She had a new best friend in Margaret, who was quite different from Bethy-Sue and Laura-Ellen. Margaret was more interested in birds than in boys.

"I've got five brothers," she told Sara, "and I know everything I need to know about boys and a lot I wish I didn't."

When Sara tried to explain that Gabriel Courbeau was a mysterious, romantic character because he was abused by his father and was sensitive and creative, Margaret said, "If I

123

didn't have more respect for birds, I'd call you a birdbrain. No boy is mysterious, and the only sensitive, romantic ones are in books."

Margaret was very positive about this, but Sara wondered how long it would be before she changed her mind and watched boys as well as birds.

In a few weeks Gabe's prediction that everyone would be wearing pants and parkas to school came true, and Sara asked Blanche to help her knit mittens, as her need for them was more immediate than the Christmas scarf intended for her father. Waiting for the bus on mornings when the sun that seeped through the trees gave only a pale light with no warmth, Sara held her books like a shield against the touchy wind.

In the barn Richard was finally chided by the sight of Sara and Kyra wearing their parkas during the evenings, so he invested in more stoves. He installed a large wood stove in the common room, fitting its insulated chimney pipe through a hole in the wall, up along the side of the barn and far enough above the roof so it would be safe to use. "I must buy some fire extinguishers," he reminded himself. "We never did get around to bulldozing a pond."

"Never mind the fire extinguishers!" Sara pleaded. "Start up a fire right now. I can't wait to get all of me warm."

"Me too," said Demetri. He trailed around in one of Richard's hooded sweatshirts, which hung halfway to his ankles. His hands never appeared out of the sleeves, and the hood was tied around his face so tightly that his features were squeezed together.

"This will be real New England heat," Ben warned. "You roast your face and freeze your butt at the same time. Or you roast your butt and freeze your face. You can't have it both ways at once."

"That's what built New England character," observed Harvey. "When people in this part of the country conserve energy, by God, it's a measure of true sacrifice. It makes you mad when the rest of the country doesn't help."

"You better not say that in Montana or Michigan or some of those other frigid places."

"You know it's Washington I'm talking about," said Harvey. "You'll all have to come visit us in Tahiti next winter, eh, Blanche?"

Blanche nodded. Harvey had brought her chaise and TV downstairs and parked them near the stove. She spent a lot of time sitting there, crocheting or watching TV or playing cribbage with Harvey, and Sara noticed that sometimes, until she caught someone looking at her, she did absolutely nothing.

Kyra came in, dragging her painting equipment, a large piece of Masonite fitted with a rope handle on which she stretched her watercolor paper, and a carpenter's toolbox in which she kept her paints and brushes. A plastic jug for water was tied to her belt, and her collapsible easel was under one arm. "Ooof!" She let things down with a thud. "That's a workout. Hi, Demi! You been a great kid today?"

He ran to her for a hug. "Your nose is cold."

"And that's not all!" Kyra held up her hands. She'd cut the thumbs and fingers off some old woolen gloves. "From now on I'll take photographs. The autumn colors are fantastic — just like you promised, Richard. It's exciting to paint outdoors, but it's damn uncomfortable. Even the marrow in my bones is frozen."

"Let me warm you up!" Richard put his arms around her and pounded her back vigorously.

She rubbed her nose against the rough wool of his shirt. "If it's this cold now, what's it going to be like in the middle of the winter?"

That ice-filled thought was one Sara tried to put down, although it didn't seem to bother the men. Ben said he'd rather work to keep warm in winter than have to work at all in summer heat. Zeke said working on his tree-trunk carvings in the yard kept him hot enough, but the problem was, "Who's going to buy them? They don't exactly fit on a mantelpiece. If I don't sell something soon, I'll head up north for some hunting."

"You might do that anyway," Richard suggested. "I'd love to taste venison again. And bear! I haven't eaten bear in years. We could fill up the freezer for the winter with a buck and a bear."

"You're counting your calories before they're bagged," Zeke said. "I'm a good shot and a good guide, but each year's different. Some you win. Some you come back empty-handed."

"I don't mind venison if I don't know I'm eating it," Blanche admitted. "Then I'm not thinking about the poor deer while I'm chewing. But bear meat doesn't appeal to me at all."

Sara agreed. "Please don't shoot a bear."

"I'm not even sure that I'll go hunting," Zeke protested. "This barn life is making me lazy."

After taking their turns at cooking and doing the kitchen cleanup chores, Sara and Gabe did their homework at the kitchen table. They kept the range mulling along with helpings of slab wood. Sara loved the coziness of sitting close to

126

Gabe. The only sounds were the crackling of a piece of wood flaring in the stove and the turning of pages in their books. Gabe helped her with social studies and math, and Sara found that not all her childhood experiences were useless, for she had absorbed and remembered the accent and rhythm of well-spoken French, and she could help Gabe, who had trouble getting the sound of his father's boyhood Canadian French out of his voice.

While they did their homework, the others listened to the news on TV. Then the men took care of what they now called "barn business": ordering supplies and paying bills and deciding on priorities like insulating the large area Zeke and Ben and Gabe slept in and giving it inner walls for privacy.

Later in the evenings, when Demetri was half asleep on the couch and Sara and Gabe had finished their school work, they listened to Richard and Harvey read aloud. Richard liked short pieces from a favorite book or a magazine; essays on words or funny anecdotes; short stories by Bret Harte or Jack London — even Robert Service poems about the Yukon he could read with hammy melodrama.

One evening Harvey brought out an old book. "I bought this years ago and always meant to read it. Richard's whale records reminded me of it. So here we go: 'Call me Ishmael. Some years ago — never mind how long precisely — having little or no money in my purse and nothing particular to interest me on shore, I thought I would sail about a little and see the watery part of the world.' I wonder if he got to Tahiti," Harvey digressed before he went on with the foreboding words that set the scene in *Moby Dick*.

On her own Sara was reading *Ivanhoe*, because Harvey came back from a flea market with a handsomely bound set of the works of Sir Walter Scott. Although the books smelled musty, the print was small, the sentences convoluted, and the dialogue seemed unnatural, Sara became fascinated with the characters and their fate, and with the life of the time, especially in castles. It occurred to her that the barn, which had so awed her when she first saw it, had become the framework of her daily life, and its huge timbers enclosed her with the same strength a castle's stones would have provided; and, in a way, the activities of her father and his friends composed an existence similar to that carried on in the confines of a feudal castle. There were the large kitchen and pantry and the storerooms filled with the garden harvest to see them through the winter. There were the craftsmen and their busy shops. There were the animals — the goats and Gabe's dog and Sara's cat, although Mickey was hardly the whippetlike dog seen in medieval tapestries and Fonzie was far from a heraldic lion.

Sara could look around at the group listening to Harvey read and pretend they were inhabitants of a castle. Richard was the king and Kyra a fitting consort. Harvey was the court scholar and magician, who should be telling tales of Arthur and his knights rather than reading about whales and whalers. Zeke, who seemed to keep more in touch with the news of the world and Martin's Corners than the rest of them did, was a troubador. Sara was a princess, of course, and Blanche her loving nurse. Ben was a knight, the gentle "parfit knight" she'd read about. And Gabe was a faithful squire. The only character they didn't seem to have was a villain. An enemy. Then she thought that perhaps Gabe's father would qualify as one. He seemed to be a villain to his sons anyway.

On an afternoon when Sara walked from the bus alone because Gabe had stayed late for a basketball game, she thought the barn looked particularly fortresslike in the shallow October light. She wondered how it would have felt centuries ago to be hurrying to reach the safety of a castle before nightfall. The fields looked empty of all life, although she knew she could sit quietly on the stone wall and before long see a chipmunk or hear a wintering towhee scratching in the bushes. The big doors by the ramp, closed now against the autumn wind, were almost as much bother to pry open as a drawbridge was to let down, so she took a path through the field, past the wood-burning kiln, and went into the barn through the pottery, which echoed with sounds. The ball-mill used for grinding glazes clanked and rattled. The clay-mixing machine thrummed and slurped. The potter's wheel purred. And through it all Richard was singing something about the sun shining in. He was so absorbed he didn't see or hear her. She felt suddenly shy of interrupting him.

On the next floor she saw Harvey bending over his jigsaw with intense concentration. He was cutting something intricate, and she had learned not to startle him. She heard Ben using his sanding machine. Upstairs she found Blanche snoozing on her chaise, and Zeke was glancing through a cookbook in the kitchen. "Do you care what you eat tonight, so long as it's hot and delicious?"

Sara looked at him warily. "As long as it isn't eel, whale, rattlesnake, or rabbit."

"You're safe." Zeke plopped browned pieces of what looked like an elongated chicken into the pot.

"What is it?" demanded Sara.

"Chop me some onions and I'll tell you."

"That's bribery."

"No. It's common sense. I'm late getting supper started."

She put down her books and lent a hand. When it was all in the pot, she said, "Okay. What is it?"

"How does goose stew sound?"

"Funny."

"Let's hope it doesn't turn out to be. That goose looked too tough to roast, so I'm stewing it. We'll call it *ragout de goose* — if anyone asks."

At supper the ragout turned into such a conversation piece, with Richard leading them through a series of culinary and cultural exchanges, that Sara had to wait for a pause to make an announcement. "Our social studies class is going to do an assembly program. We have three groups and each one has to write and put on a one-act play and I'm the chairperson of our group. I have to direct it all. It has to be about something medieval."

When Worthington had announced medieval life as the topic, Sara had looked up with a grin. Her reading of *Ivanhoe* might not be wasted after all. Amid all the noncommittal expressions, her lone gleam of interest didn't escape the teacher's eye. He named her chairperson of Group A, and she was responsible for seeing that Rob Luther, Ziggy Gignoux, Yvonne Courbeau, Matthew Hobner, Jason Purvey, Glenna Johnson, Margaret Allen, and Cherylene Benedetto each picked a character to play and worked out a plot and wrote dialogue together — and rehearsed the result.

"How about holding a tournament?" Richard suggested.

"With horses? And armor? And lists? And onlookers? And canopies? On a small stage? We're only eighth-graders." Sara felt almost indignant at such an extravagant, impossible suggestion.

"So? That shouldn't stop you." Richard laughed at himself.

"The horses might be difficult. But go to it, Sara. You ought to be able to do something interesting with the medieval life, by golly."

"Don't worry," said Sara. "If you can make a stew out of a goose, I guess you can make a play out of a bunch of people in a castle. Nothing to it."

# 10

"I should never have looked Worthington in the eye when he brought up putting on a play," Sara complained to Gabe. "Then he would have picked someone else to be chairperson of our group. Maybe Vonnie. She's bossy enough to make people do things. I'm not."

"Vonnie would have told him exactly where to go before he had a chance to put her in charge of anything."

The bus, which seemed to have developed a mechanical bronchitis, coughed to a stop at the Courbeaus' lane, where Elise waited. Yvonne was fifty paces or so from the road, moving slowly. She didn't look up and she didn't move any faster when the driver impatiently blew the horn, which had a nasal honk that matched the catarrhal condition of the bus. Yvonne hauled herself on board and slumped into the first empty place. Elise had already settled into a seat in front of Gabe and turned to talk with him.

"What's the matter with Vonnie?" he asked.

"What else — it's Pa. He's in one of his terrible spells — sitting smack in front of the TV, drinking beer and bashing anybody who goes near him. Even Francie. He landed one on Vonnie and she swears she'll get him next time. She'll belt him back."

"Then he'll really hurt her — like he did me." Gabe jumped up and went to sit with Yvonne. He seemed to be doing all the talking — earnestly. She nodded several times and then said something in a furious voice that upset Gabe. When he came back, Sara asked, "Is she all right?"

"Her arm is bruised and sore. She's mostly mad. Mad at Papa and mad at me for leaving home, because she's the one he goes for now."

"I'm sorry she's having a tough time. Everything seems to be hard for her. I haven't been able to get her to help with the play. I don't think she likes me at all."

"She's beginning to get to me too. She seems to think we have a glamorous life at the barn and none of us ever does any work. She's trying to make me feel guilty because I left home, and I told her if I had to live at home there's no way I could have any privacy and study. She thinks I'm weird because I want to do well in school." He slid down in the seat and half closed his eyes, as if he were tired and discouraged. "I told her she ought to complain to someone about Papa's hitting her, but I guess she's as scared to do it as I was. And who would you tell?"

"The police?" Sara asked. "What would happen if you did?"

"I don't know. He'd probably get wild if he thought anyone was interfering with him. He might walk out on all of them

— he's threatened to once or twice — and then I'd have to go home to help with the wood and the animals. I don't want to think about it."

"Why doesn't your mother complain?"

"I've wondered about that. She used to try to stop him beating on Alphie and Giles. Now I think she's too tired to do anything but try not to get beaten up herself."

As they left the bus and went to cope with clattering lockers and chattering friends, Sara realized her problem with Group A's play was nothing compared to the Courbeaus' everyday drama.

It did, however, present difficulties. Worthington gave them only half a class period to organize their plays. Among the girls Cherylene won the part of the queen through her refusal to consider any lower station. Glenna gave in when Sara suggested she be a sorceress, even though Sara thought Glenna, with her large popping eyes and unnatural ash-blonde hair, was hardly a sorcerly type. Margaret, who was used to compromise as a means of survival with her brothers, said she'd just as soon be a lady-in-waiting, and Yvonne could be a princess.

"I don't want to be any princess," Yvonne announced. "That would make me sick. And I mean throw-up sick."

As chairperson, Sarah had to avoid any such performance. "Then Margaret will be a princess, and you can think about what you want to be and tell me next meeting."

Of the boys only Rob Luther took himself and his school work seriously. He chose to be a knight like Galahad. The others said they'd think about it, although Ziggy Gignoux seemed to agree with Yvonne that the whole idea was nauseating.

After that first meeting, when it became evident that a certain amount of positive thought and hard work would have to be involved in their production, Sara found she wasn't receiving help from anyone but Rob. He wrote out some speeches he wanted to say, and Sara found them so full of old-fashioned words she couldn't understand them. "Are you sure people talked like this?"

"They do in the King Arthur book I have. It's by a guy named Howard Pyle. They sound real formal with each other."

"Then maybe that's just how he thought they ought to sound. We're supposed to tell about how people lived. We're not supposed to make people guess what we're talking about."

Sara found to her dismay that Rob's capacity to take criticism was limited. "You do it then," he said and walked off in a most un-Galahad-like dudgeon.

None of them wanted to meet after school because that meant waiting for the late bus. The boys were also concerned with the intramural basketball tournament.

When Worthington asked Sara how Group A was doing, she didn't want to admit that they weren't doing anything. She listened to the other groups, and when she heard that the B's were having a planning party at someone's house and the C's were doing the same, she asked her father if she could invite the group to the barn.

"How about late Sunday afternoon?" Richard suggested. "Kyra and I could provide a high tea."

"Can I tell them doughnuts and cider? High tea would scare them off."

"Whatever you call it, we'll do it. If they can arrive on their own, I'll drive them home."

Sara fidgeted on Sunday, wondering if any of them would come. She sat up in her room, where she could hear a car drive

up, and felt as if she were trapped in a play within a play —
as if she were a forlorn princess in a tower, waiting for rescue.
About four o'clock a station wagon brought Cherylene and
Margaret, and she rushed down to escort them through the
barn. Margaret had visited Sara several times and each time
had said living in a barn was beautiful compared to living with
five brothers. It was Cherylene's first visit, and Sara suddenly
saw the barn anew, with the other girl's disdainful eyes.

"Don't pay any attention to this stuff," Sara said, leading
them past the piles of oddments that strewed the middle floor
of the barn. "Upstairs it's more like a house."

"It's crazy!" exclaimed Margaret, "but I love it." Cherylene,
even when she saw the common room with the three couches
and the wood stove and the Ping-Pong and pool tables, didn't
love it. She looked uncomfortable and kept her coat on. Finally everyone but Yvonne had arrived, and Sara suggested
they sit around the kitchen table. The doughnuts and cider
disappeared faster than the ideas and dialogue appeared. Rob
and Sara were the only ones who'd read anything beyond their
school text about castles, and the others' ideas must have come
from Saturday morning TV cartoons. Cherylene acted bored.
Ziggy wanted to go into the other room and watch the basketball game on TV, and Matthew and Glenna were more interested in making the seven o'clock movie in Martin's Corners.
They kept looking at their watches and pretending to be in
keeping with medieval times by making remarks about the
sand running out in their hourglasses.

Sara stared at a piece of paper on which she'd printed
Jason Purvey's contribution of a title for their skit, *Meanwhile,
Back at the Castle* — and under that: characters — Queen,
Cherylene; King, Jason; Princess, Margaret; Knight, Rob;

Court Astrologer and Magician, Matthew; Sorceress, Glenna; Guard, Ziggy; Cook, Sara. Yvonne was declared lady-in-waiting by default. Cherylene insisted the queen needed one, and Yvonne wasn't there to protest.

"That's a lot of people. How can we get anything dramatic out of them?" Sara asked.

"Or funny?" added Jason.

Sara didn't even mind when Richard came in to make his afternoon brew of Red Zinger tea and honey and sensed their lack of progress and their lack of hope. "Mind if I interrupt?" He pulled up a chair. "I have a thing about castles. Sara, do you remember the castle at Turku? In Finland?"

"No." She hadn't ever mentioned at Northwoods Regional School that she'd ever been anywhere else but in Yellow Creek, Tennessee. Rob stared at her, and even Cherylene looked impressed.

"That could be. You were only three years old. Well, it's an enormous castle. It's like a whole village inside the walls — a village with blacksmith shops and stables and kitchens and storerooms and a great hall and a chapel and dungeons —"

He caught them up with his descriptions until he had them listening for the ring of horses' hoofs on cobblestones in the courtyard, peering down through the iron-barred grill in the floor into a well-like dungeon, awed by the gilded carvings in the chapel. He led them along the ramparts and let them feel why the castle was so important to the history of Sweden and Finland. "Now you know what can go on inside a castle, just brainstorm your characters into it." Richard persuaded them it was as easy as that and walked out.

Sara hoped for once that his kind of magic would work, and it did. They changed their cast so Matthew was a prisoner

136

instead of a court magician, and plot and action began to take shape. Sara thought of a way that the cook's part could be crucial in rescuing the prisoner, who would turn out to be a double spy.

"We can put in lots of fighting," Matthew pointed out. "Fighting cuts down on dialogue. You just thrust with a sword and grunt a lot."

"What about costumes?" asked Cherylene, whose main interest was clothes.

"Ugh. I hate to sew," said Glenna.

"We'd better do something," said Sara. "The B's are doing the Crusades and they're making shields and swords out of cardboard and spray-painting them. And the C's are doing a trial scene for Joan of Arc."

"They wanted to burn her at the stake, but Worthie canned it," Ziggy reported.

"Come on, you guys," Jason urged. "Think. Speak. We've got to say something."

Slowly they put down a series of lines, some contributed by Jason who wanted to be funny, some by Rob who wanted to be serious, some by Cherylene who wanted to be glamorous, and some by Matthew who wanted to be dramatic. Sara wrote speeches down as fast as she could.

It was at this point that Yvonne arrived, with no apology for being late. She sat down, didn't take her parka off, and scowled. "What do I have to do? It better be a good part or I won't bother to come to school that day."

"Then Worthie will flunk you for the project," Rob said.

"So? All this stuff about how people lived years ago is a waste."

Sara felt the enthusiasm that had been so hard to build

among the others drifting away. Yvonne was going to hail on their parade unless someone could change her attitude. "We've saved a good part for you. You can be brave and heroic. You're the cook and you rescue the prisoner from his dungeon."

Margaret started to say, "But that's your —" and caught Sara's frantic look.

"Vonnie's going to be the cook, right?" Sara emphasized. "After all, I can be the lady-in-waiting. Or we could write her out and I'll be the announcer and the prompter. We'll need an announcer to set the scene because we'll have to pretend the scenery and most of the props."

Sara thought being the announcer who could read from a paper would be safer than speaking lines, with the chance her mind might go blank, but Yvonne thought that Sara had given up an important role, letting her be the cook, so she accepted it with a bit of a gloat.

"Good," said Sara. "That's all we can do today. My father'll drive you home when you're ready to go."

On her way out, Yvonne saw Gabe and Zeke playing pool. She stopped to watch, and Gabe asked, "How's it going?"

"This dumb play? Or home?"

"Both."

She didn't answer his questions. She challenged him. "Why don't you come home and find out?"

After Yvonne left, Sara asked, "Why did she bother to come at all?"

"Curiosity probably. Now I bet she'll go home and tell Papa I was playing pool."

When Richard returned from dropping the kids off, he was enthusiastic about the play and the actors. "That Rob's an eager lad. I gave him an idea or two, and he's going to add

138

them to the script. By golly gee, I don't want to miss seeing this production! You're going to put on a great medieval spy story. You'll have the kids on the edge of their seats."

"I wouldn't count on it." Sara tried to damp his enthusiasm because she didn't dare count on it herself. "Besides, it's only a school assembly. Parents aren't invited."

"More's the pity!" said Richard. "The whole thing could be extremely entertaining." Sara didn't care for either his tone of voice or his chuckle.

Every day she checked on whether the kids were learning their lines or not. It was mostly not. And Rob, who knew his lines and everyone else's, kept wanting to pad his part and changed his lines, which mixed up everyone's cues.

Jason said, "I know about what the words are, but I'm trying to milk them for laughs, so they don't always come out the same."

Cherylene hadn't learned her part because she was making her costume — it was going to be trimmed with genuine fake ermine — and Margaret said she was trying to learn her part, but she wasn't good at memorizing. Glenna insisted the sorceress should only move around mysteriously and recite spells and incantations.

"If I can't remember my lines, I'll start a fight," Matthew promised. Ziggy wanted to drop out because he'd made his class basketball team and wanted time to practice. No one seemed to have a mutual time for rehearsals. Sara asked them to come to the barn again on Sunday, but only Rob, Cherylene, Margaret, and Jason showed up. The assembly was to be on the following Thursday. Doomsday, Sara thought.

On Monday, when Sara followed Yvonne off the bus, she asked, "Do you know your lines yet?"

139

"Who cares? As long as I do what I'm supposed to do with that grill? The others all know what I'm doing."

"I care!" Sara felt her face and her temper heat up. "If you don't say the right words, they won't know what to say back. That's what cues are all about. It matters a lot what you say."

"Come off it. No one really cares but you and Rob and Worthington."

"It'll be in front of the whole eighth grade."

"So hurray. The only things the school cares about are the football games, the hockey games, and the basketball games."

With such a lack of cooperation from the cast, Sara had only to think of the play to break into a cold sweat and feel dizzy. After a dismal run-through during their lunch hour, she wanted to tell Worthington that her group wouldn't be ready on Thursday. They might never be ready. No one knew or kept to the lines. Only Cherylene and Margaret had costumes, and the boys absolutely refused to wear turtlenecks and tights. "No way!" they had agreed in an angry chorus.

Rob wasn't in school Tuesday, and Sara found he was out sick with a strep throat. He phoned her after school and whispered, "I'll be there Thursday. Or else."

"Or else what!" Sara moaned. She hung up, hoping he wouldn't be able to make it and that would mean they could postpone or even drop the whole mess. Twice during supper Sara stopped eating and stared at her plate in what seemed to be a state of bewilderment.

"Are you worried about something, Sara?" Kyra asked. "Or not feeling well? You look like Demetri when he's coming down with a fever — "

Sara brightened up. A fever would solve everything. She

wouldn't show up and that would definitely be that. No announcer, no prompter, no producer could equal no show.

Gabe said, "I hear we get to see your show. All the junior high classes. It's the first assembly in weeks. Worthington must think you're really terrific."

"You'll be there?" Sara was sure she was going to be ill. She had thought it was to be an assembly for just her grade.

"You borrowed some things from my chest for Margaret, but you never came back to find a costume for yourself," Blanche reminded her.

"I'm not wearing a costume. I'm announcing the play and telling about the scenery you're supposed to imagine and who the characters are. That's all. I maybe ought to look nice, but I'm not going to dress up particularly."

"I have just the thing!" exclaimed Kyra. "It's a dress that would look a lot better on you than it ever did on me."

Upstairs, Kyra held up a dress of cornflower-blue wool that had a pattern of scrolled white embroidery around the neck. "That's a warm blue. With your reddish hair so full of gold highlights, it should be a perfect complement."

Sara put it on, and Kyra squinted at her in a painterly way. "I haven't painted a portrait for a couple of years, but the way you look in that dress makes me want to try. Will you pose for me? If it turns out well, we could surprise Richard with it for Christmas."

"All right." Sara liked the color and the cloth. It felt like wearing a piece of warm blue sky.

On Wednesday Worthington had promised the groups run-through time on the stage during their class period, and Sara hoped he would see with his own eyes and hear with his own ears that Group A's production was not ready for public view, especially with Rob out sick. But when the class came into the auditorium they discovered that the seventh-grade chorus was shrilling away, rehearsing for parents' night, and Miss Dodds refused to relinquish the stage. "You can find corners for your groups. I cannot move the piano."

Worthington apologized and deployed the actors back to the classroom and the corridor outside for their run-through. Then he misjudged his time and spent most of it coaching Group C's battle techniques so they wouldn't maim each other.

"Sorry, Sara," he said, "but as I remember your script, you shouldn't have any technical problems. No battles — "

"There's a fight!" Matthew reminded him.

"Then don't really hit each other with anything and you'll be okay. Just make a lot of noise. And you all know your parts — "

"Oh sure!" said Jason. Unfortunately Worthington didn't recognize his tone of voice to mean that they sure didn't.

"Mr. Worthington — " began Sara, ready to plead for postponement, when the bell rang. The teacher was the first one out of the room.

# 11

Sara dressed as fearfully as if she were preparing to be executed on that Thursday morning. As she put on the blue dress, she hoped it would add some of Kyra's energy and strength of purpose to carry her through the day's ordeal.

Blanche stopped her in the hall. "Here's my rhinestone brooch. That dress is sweet but it hasn't much zip to it."

Sara gripped the brooch which, to her dismay, seemed to be as large and brilliant as a light bulb.

"That's a lucky brooch," Blanche underlined. "Here, let me pin it on for you."

Sara realized Blanche had made an effort to rise early and see her off to school with a talisman. She let her pin it onto the scrolled embroidery and hoped Kyra wouldn't be horrified at the effect. She tried to thank Blanche with some enthusiasm.

In the kitchen Ben dished up a large plate of oatmeal, added cream and brown sugar, and put it on the table in front of her. "Eat hearty. Oatmeal has seen strong men through battles. It's kept the Scots feisty for centuries."

Richard arrived in the kitchen, wearing his parka. "Would you like me to drive you and Gabe to school this morning?"

"No!" Sara could feel an odd little balloon of panic, like a bubble of gum, right under her rib cage. "I mean, thanks, but the bus will be fine, won't it, Gabe?" She was afraid if Richard delivered them to the door, he'd invent a reason to stay around and watch the assembly. Then she remembered that because grades seven, eight, and nine were included, the assembly would be held during the last two periods of the day. "The assembly isn't until after lunch. So you wouldn't want to wait around all day just to see our twenty-minute play."

"You impugn my motives!" Richard pretended to be cross. "I wasn't trying to insinuate myself into the audience. I simply offered you a lift because I'll be driving past the school on my way to Berwick to pick up some glazing materials. Now, once again, would you care for a ride?"

"Yes I would." Sara changed her mind as she realized she didn't want to be on a noisy bus.

"Fine. I'm ready when you're ready."

Zeke saluted her with a wave of his spoon. "Break a leg, Sara! That's wishing you good luck, you know."

"I'm glad you explained."

"We'll be waiting to hear all about it at supper," Harvey assured her. Demetri gave her a sleepy hug.

It was comforting to know they all cared. She put on her parka and a knitted hat as if they were armor and her mittens as if they were gauntlets. She was even glad of Blanche's lucky brooch.

The first person Sara saw at school, waiting for her in the lobby, was Rob. Her relief dissolved when he spoke in a whisper. "I think I can do it, but I'm saving my voice. I'm not going to talk in any of my classes."

Sara didn't have much to say in her classes either, nor at lunch. The bubble under her rib cage grew larger. She didn't feel like eating. Their social studies class came next, and Worthington told them to meet in the backstage area. Those needing to put on costumes received a pass from him to change in the first-floor lavatories. Gradually Sara's group assembled, and Sara saw what they had come up with for costumes.

Jason, the king, had on the tightest pair of jeans he could move in and fur-trimmed boots that looked as if they belonged to his mother, as did his purple velvet blouse and shiny glass jewelry. Cherylene had made him a crown to match hers out of gold-sprayed cardboard. She wore a long, blue brocade dress cuffed with lace, edged at the bottom with orlon ermine, and topped with a feather boa. It would have been perfect, Sara thought, if she were going to do her part as a takeoff, but Cherylene didn't possess a sense of humor. She was playing it straight. Margaret wore a long skirt and a sweater with gold embroidery and a junior-sized crown, again courtesy of Cherylene. Matthew, the spy-prisoner, had on his usual Saturday clothing, a patched jacket and patched pants, and was barefoot. He was busily smudging his face with makeup Yvonne had brought. That was her only contribution — that and the fact that she'd worn a long green dress instead of jeans and sweater. Ziggy, the guard, wore his usual school clothes — chinos and a fake letter sweater.

"You don't look medieval!" Sara told him.

"I could get my sweat suit from my gym locker, if that's any better."

"A guard wouldn't wear sweat pants," objected Cherylene. She was mad because the others hadn't bothered to find costumes. "You could at least have tried to find something."

"I didn't have time. And you look like a — "

145

"Where's Worthington?" Sara interrupted, trying to keep a fight between the queen and the guard from breaking out before they even got on stage.

Rob had his coat on and was shivering. "Do you feel all right?" Sara asked him.

"Just — nerves." His teeth chattered. "Vonnie, can I use some of your makeup?"

"Help yourself. Or let me help you. I love to fool around with makeup." It was unusual for Yvonne to offer anything, so Sara thought perhaps something was going right, until Jason said, "Rob's put in new lines for himself again. He seems to think they'll work out with the old cues, and you're supposed to use his script to prompt with. He's been lying in bed two days — *fattening his part!*"

"Oh." Sara felt as if her head and her toes had no connection — as if all of her body in between was missing.

Margaret came up. "I can't remember one of my lines, not one."

"Neither can I!" said Glenna, her eyes popping out more than ever.

"Fake it," said Jason. "Rob's going to screw us up anyway. Improvise. Like they do on 'Saturday Night Live.' "

"My mother won't let me watch that show," said Cherylene. "This is going to be awful." She did look white. "I feel faint, Sara. I don't think I can say anything. Couldn't I just kind of walk around and not say anything?"

"You know what the trouble is?" Matthew looked around at the group. "We don't know our lines and we haven't rehearsed this thing enough. None of us know what we're doing or what anyone else is doing!" He looked awed at his analysis. And then worried.

"I've been trying to tell you that for two weeks!" Sara was cold and then hot. Her stomach reappeared in her middle and made her feel queasy. "Do you want to do this? Or shall we tell Mr. Worthington we can't go on?"

"We want out," said Jason. "You tell him."

"Me?" Sara asked.

"You're the chairperson."

Worthington was sipping distractedly from a styrofoam cup of cold coffee when Sara approached him. "Well, now! Group B's all set and ready to go. So is Group C. You A's should, by alphabetical standards, go first. How about it? Everything ready?"

"No," said Sara. "Nothing's ready. We don't want to go on first or second or last. Please can we drop out? I couldn't get the kids to learn their lines and rehearse. It's going to be awful and we'll look so dumb. Couldn't you have just the other two groups?"

"And leave twenty minutes of an assembly in front of three grades with nothing to fill it? No way, as you all say." Sara thought that Worthington, if he was so keen on medieval life, ought to be able to fill the time by talking about it, but she didn't dare say so. "Come, come. It can't be that bad, Sara."

"Then can we go on last? Ziggy needs time to get his sweat suit from the gym. He looks all wrong in a letter sweater."

"Good heavens!" Worthington at least found the idea of a letter sweater in medieval times funny. He giggled nervously. "All right. The B's will go first. But you be next. I promised the C's they'd be last. They have a real grand finale to their play."

All Sara could do was nod and hope the numbness seeping through her would last until the play was over. Bells rang.

Feet scuffed, shuffled, and stamped as classes filed toward the auditorium. Hinges squeaked and seats banged down. The swell of voices rose with a zoolike roar until Mr. Worthington went before the curtain to announce that this afternoon his eighth-grade social studies class was going to entertain and educate the school with three plays of their own writing to illustrate the highlights of medieval life. The first would be about the trial of Joan of Arc, as it would have been reported and broadcast by a TV studio, complete with "man-on-the-street" interviews, ha-ha. A real remote — get it? Remote broadcast, ha-ha-ha.

Sara knew the B Group had a great time putting their skit together, and the cast thought it was funny and loved doing it. The audience laughed all through it — despite poor Joan's tragedy and discomfort — and there were cheers and whistles at the end. While they were taking a curtain call, Worthington signaled to Sara.

"You're introducing the play, right? Then as soon as the B's are off and you A's are on stage, you step through the curtain and do your announcer thing."

Sara put her hand in the pocket of her dress and pulled out a piece of Kleenex. She stared at it, felt in the pocket again, and realized with dread that she didn't have her paper with the introduction carefully printed on it in large letters. She remembered sticking it into her pocket when she dressed that morning, and then remembered what else she'd done with it — propped it up on the shelf above the bathroom sink when she was brushing her teeth and fixing her hair. She'd wanted to read it over one more time. Then Gabe had banged on the door and told her it was late, and she'd rushed out and forgotten it.

148

The room about her seemed to close in and then the walls seemed to rush away. She felt as frightened as she did in her worst nightmares, and she couldn't even scream and wake up.

"I've lost my paper!" She pulled at Worthington's sleeve. "I don't know what to say. I can't do it."

"Read it from the script. Isn't that your script on the prompter's stool there?"

Sara picked it up. "This is one Rob rewrote. He left off my introduction. I don't know where the other scripts are."

"Then just *tell* about the scene and who the characters arc. Okay, A's. On stage!"

The B's came hustling off, hugging each other and slapping backs and hey-heying with relief. It was over and they were a success.

The A's struggled on stage. Rob still wore his coat and looked as if he were frozen. When Sara yelled, "Take it off!" at him, he looked confused and stood there, clearing his throat. Voices in the auditorium buzzed again, like a big electric bug-zapper, Sara thought, that was waiting out there to zap her. Worthington pointed to the middle of the curtain. "Go, go, go!"

"Go where?" Sara muttered. She couldn't find the parting of the curtains. She pushed against them, and they billowed away from her, bulging out toward the auditorium. It must have looked funny to the audience to see someone behind the curtains trying to find the way out, and kids giggled with each surge of the material. Her hand suddenly slipped through and she had to follow it.

Before her, faces made rows like waves coming from a great distance. They were going to rise up in a gigantic crest and thunder down on her with a ferocious roar. As always in a crisis, Sara had to go to the bathroom, and it seemed as if she could only concentrate on not letting that happen. The only words in her head seemed to be, "I will not pee."

Instead of the ferocious roar she expected, there was a hush — a frightening silence as the multitude of faces waited for her to say something. She felt as if her throat had become a dry stick, and she had no power to strike a sound from it.

In the wings Worthington realized she was transfixed with stage fright and prompted in a loud whisper, "Tell the name of the play. And the characters. And then get off." There were loud guffaws from kids in the front rows who could hear him.

Sara obediently opened her mouth. "The name of our play —" came out in a high squeak such as she'd never uttered before, like an LP revved up to a higher speed. Or someone who'd taken a lungful of helium. More kids snickered.

She wanted to step back through the curtain and disappear. She couldn't, because she'd let go of the edges. She'd have to push at them until she found the opening again, offering more opportunities for laughter. She had to go on. Somehow she brought her voice down an octave. "The name of our play is *Meanwhile, Back at the Castle*." She named the characters and the actors, batted at the curtain, and remembered she hadn't set the scene. So she turned around and said, "Our play takes place in a castle." More laughter, and she failed to see the humor in it.

Worthington suddenly pulled the curtains; the heavy velvet jerked and swung past her, throwing out a haze of dust. Sara sneezed. She followed the curtain into the wings, sneezing and sneezing. She gasped for breath. Her eyes ran. She knew she had to reach the girls' room before something else ran. She bolted past the teacher and into the corridor and made the bathroom just in time.

She didn't want to go back to the stage, but she remembered Worthington holding out Rob's script to her as she fled past. At least she had an idea of what the actors were supposed to be doing and saying, and he didn't. She couldn't let her group down, even if she never wanted to see any of them again.

She slipped back into the wings and stood by Worthington. There was a large silence going on as the cast stared at each other with a "What's next? Who's next?" look of panic. Sara didn't even know where they were in the script, and Matthew couldn't start a fight for diversion because he was supposedly still down in the dungeon. Rob, who had so elaborated his part, tried to start up the dialogue and did a speech over again. The audience was aware of his repetition, and there were a few titters.

Worthington handed Sara the script. "You prompt. They must be around here. I've got to check on the last group."

"He's abandoning me," thought Sara. "He doesn't want to have anything to do with this mess."

She found what Rob was saying, and once more, when he stopped, no one said a word. He hadn't used the old cues at all, and Jason didn't realize it was his turn to speak. Sara hissed, "Jason! Say 'We must have a traitor in our midst.' "

He didn't hear her. She called out louder, "Jason! Say 'We must have a traitor in our midst!' "

Jason turned toward her and, meaning to ask if it was his turn, pointed to himself and mouthed, "Who — me?" The audience roared. Jason tried to lessen the confusion. "I'm no traitor," he said, and forgot to go on then with what he was supposed to say.

Rob, however, after rewriting his part so much, remembered what Jason should say and took over. "We must have a traitor in our midst," and went on with another plummy rant he'd added to his part. Glenna, whose apparel had been converted from her cousin's belly-dancing costume, filled another pause with one of her sorcerer's incantations. As it didn't make sense anyway, it didn't really matter where she put it in. Sara suddenly focused on Rob and saw he was still wearing his overcoat, which had a large fur collar, and the only other things that showed were his bright red stockings and furry bedroom slippers. Then she realized the furred coat was the main part of his costume because they'd read about how important fur was, not only to keep people warm, but as a sign of their wealth. As for his face, she wondered if he had looked at himself when Yvonne had finished his makeup. It was chalk-white with black circles around his eyes, black shadows on his cheeks, and a black widow's peak of hair grease-painted into his hair line. He looked like a punk rock star. Sara wondered why she hadn't realized before how bizarre he looked. Probably she'd been too frantic over discovering she didn't have her introduction in hand to read.

Cherylene pulled her brocade train and took another pose, as if she were a fashion model. Matthew grew tired of waiting to be released from his dungeon — behind a box on the floor — and slowly pushed a hand into view on top of the box. It looked like one of those joke hands that crawl out from under a box lid. The audience whooped. Matthew pulled his hand out of sight.

Jason heard Rob finish another speech and saw Sara point

at him and in a frenzy of ad-libbing burst out, "This is no laughing matter — " and then began to laugh himself. Everything suddenly struck him as hilarious, and he was caught in one of those spasms of belly laughter that can't be cut off, even though he tried. Matthew, still supposedly out of sight, began to giggle and roll around. His legs flopped into view. Yvonne decided if her part was going to be worth anything at all she'd better do it quickly, so she walked over and removed the box, letting the spy-prisoner into the scene well before his time. Margaret stood there with tears in her eyes, and Sara couldn't tell if she was laughing or crying. It turned out to be laughing, and she was helpless to control it. Glenna, thinking action might help, tried a few motions that were more suited to her costume's original use.

At that point the kids in the audience began to roll in their seats, hooting and bellowing with laughter. It spread in bursts through the auditorium like a contagious plague. Worthington heard it from backstage and rushed into the wings to see Group A demoralized either by panic or inane guffaws, and the entire audience lost in gusts of laughter. Sara gave him an agonized look. "I can't tell them what to say. Or do. It's all messed up. We can't finish it. Can you pull the curtains?"

"Of course you can finish it!" Worthington couldn't acknowledge defeat. "Who has the next lines?"

"No one!" Sara insisted. "No one can say anything that would make sense now."

At that point Cherylene took a regal step toward center stage, her head lurched forward, her crown fell off, and she slid to the floor in a faint. Worthington pulled the curtain.

While Cherylene was the center of concern, Sara went to her locker, put on her parka, hat, and mittens, and walked out.

# 12

Sara stalked across the football field and into the woods. She didn't want anyone to see her, and before long several of the school buses would pass her if she walked home by the road. She knew there was a path through the trees that some of the Martin's Corners kids used. She followed it until she came to where the well-trodden way led down to the village and a less-used path continued on in the direction she hoped led homeward.

All that filled her mind was a replay of her failure in producing *Meanwhile, Back at the Castle*, and she wished she could shake it out of her head. When she couldn't, when all she could see was the exasperated red face of Mr. Worthington and all she could hear were the titters, snickers, and guffaws of the audience — and the cast! — she sat down on a rock and cried until her chest ached.

When she realized her feet were icy, her crying had turned into occasional quivering gasps. It was going to be painful to see Gabe, to hear what he thought of the fiasco, but at least her father had not been in the audience. This time he had not actually watched her mess up. Not that there was much consolation in that, but it did help to get her on her feet and walking again.

She found that the path soon disappeared under a pile of rusty beer cans. She didn't want to go back to the village and the road, so she climbed the steep slope ahead of her, hoping to find a path, or at least a view of where she was, at the top.

The trees were dense, and it was a hard climb. Bushes scratched at her. A low limb caught her hat and plucked it off. She stepped into a hole and twisted her ankle. Briars reached for her woolen dress and snagged it; cockleburrs stuck to it. At the top the underbrush was still so thick she could only keep on fighting her way branch by branch through it.

Sara knew that she had less than two hours to find her way out of the woods before twilight settled in. Her runaway mood of anger and frustration and embarrassment, which had sent her rushing out of the school, turned to a shiver of fear. What if she couldn't find her way out of the woods? What if she were lost when it became dark? She tried not to run in panic, but to walk sensibly and to keep the sun on her left, hoping she was headed north. Once she heard from far off the whine of a chain saw. Other than that she could have been the only person in the world. Even the birds were quiet, except for an occasional shriek from a blue jay.

She thought she had been in the woods for several hours when she came to a brook. It was an earnest stream, pouring itself noisily down its stony course, and Sara felt its sound was almost like having a companion. She followed it, stepping over moss-slippery rocks and punky fallen logs, even though it led east, turning its back on the fading sun, which dimmed with each wink through the trees. Sara hoped it was the brook which, eventually, bordered a large swamp beside the road.

The sun had disappeared and shadows had woven themselves into gray twilight when the rocks and logs by the stream gave way to clumps of sedge and patches of mud, and she stepped out of the trees at last. Her feet were soaked from slipping into the brook, and her clothes were soggy with sweat from her exertions. She felt weak and chilled. She wondered if she had strength enough to slog through the swamp. Yet when she saw the headlights of a car curving through the dim distance, she began to run, stumbling and sliding, toward the road. She knew where she was. The barn was about three miles away.

Gran had once made her, holding her Sunday School Bible, swear a lifetime promise never to hitchhike — but Sara prayed for another car to come. When she felt the solid macadam underfoot, she limped along until a truck rattled up to her. "Want a lift?"

A man leaned over to open the door on her side, and as the cab light went on, Sara saw it was Mr. Courbeau. Never mind what Gabe said about his father! At least she knew who he was. "Please. I do need a lift." She had just enough energy left to pull herself up onto the seat.

"You miss the school bus?"

"Yes." Sara certainly had missed the school bus.

"The way you look you must have had a hard time at school."

"It was a bad day."

"Most days are not good ones." His speech wasn't slurred, and he spoke with his strange formality, but from the way he let the truck wander over the double yellow line in the middle of the road Sara realized he was drunk. Instead of slowing down when the headlights of an oncoming car dazzled his eyes, he speeded up, and the car slewed by with a protesting blare of its horn. Sara was thoroughly scared.

As the turnoff to the Courbeaus' place came into sight she said, "I'll walk from here. Thanks for the lift." She tried to find the door handle.

Mr. Courbeau, however, reached across her and grabbed the handle himself, holding it. "I know who you are. You're that Bradford girl who lives in the barn. I met you once. Remember? In the general store? You don't want to walk the rest of the way now, do you? I wouldn't want you to. Not on a raw night like this. Not a nice little girl like you." His hand slid off the door handle and rested on her thigh. She felt as if each of his bony fingers was burning a mark through her dress to her skin.

A sudden burst of fright charged her nerves and set her heart banging. She wriggled away from him and this time grasped the door handle before he could.

"Don't get nervous," he told her, putting both his hands on the wheel and laughing, but he speeded up the truck enough so Sara knew she would be stupid to jump out. "You don't need to be afraid of an old man like me. I have a daughter your age. Name of Yvonne Celeste."

"I know Vonnie." If she kept him talking, perhaps he'd keep both his hands on the wheel.

"And you know my son Gabriel, who deserted me. That Gabriel! It's time he came home and gave me a hand. When he ran away last spring, I let him off easy. Didn't even report him as a runaway, let alone go get him and straighten him out. He's a *delinquent*, you know." Courbeau said the word with precision. "I didn't fuss because I thought he'd learn

157

what it is to work hard, and I thought he had enough family loyalty to send home some of his pay. Now Vonnie says he don't do much over there. Just runs errands for your father and sits around making dishes. Easy life. He plays pool, she says. Goes out and spends his money in a pool hall, does he!"

"No he doesn't!" Sara exclaimed. "He plays pool, but the table's right in our common room and they play for fun. And Gabe works hard. He throws good pots, my father says. It may look easy but it isn't. And he splits wood for the big kiln and helps fire it. That's real hard work."

"Well I need Gabe to split wood for me. I got orders to fill and I got a bad back and can't do it myself. I'll drop you off, little girl, and I'll get that Gabriel and bring him back where he belongs. He can work for his own father."

Courbeau's foot jammed onto the gas pedal. The truck whipped along, swaying from side to side, and then took a wild curve onto the driveway leading to the barn.

Sara planned to leap out ahead of Courbeau. She wanted to warn Gabe to stay out of sight. As she was wondering what the quickest way into the barn would be, the doors by the ramp were pushed open and Richard's truck drove out. Tires shrieked as the drivers of both trucks, blinded by the duel of headlights, suddenly braked. Sara jumped out, landed unevenly, and fell. Ben, who had been by the doors, saw her and strode to pick her up. "Here's Sara!"

Ben set her on her feet as Richard reached her and asked with considerable anxiety, "Are you all right? We were starting out to search for you." Gabe and Harvey, equipped with flashlights, came toward her too. Zeke leaned out of the truck cab.

"I'm not hurt," Sara assured them. "I walked home —

158

through the woods. It took hours. Oh, Richard! Everything's been so awful!"

"As long as you're home safe, that's all that counts. Who brought you?"

"Gabe's father. Oh! Gabe!"

She was too late. Courbeau already had a grip on his son's arm. "Come to take you home," he said. "Get in my truck. Now."

Gabe pushed his father's hand away and upset his balance. The man fell against the truck. "Don't you raise your hand to me," Courbeau said. "You should respect your father. You should do what I tell you."

"No way!" said Gabe, standing very straight and looking down at his father's slack face. "I don't respect you so I won't take orders from you. Not when you beat up your own kids — even Vonnie now — and are mean to Mama. I like my work here and I like to live here. If you try to make me come home, I'll tell everybody about all the times you've beaten me up. Nobody will want to buy eggs and chickens and wood from old man Courbeau anymore. They'll know what a rotten old man you really are."

Mr. Courbeau pulled himself upright. Maybe he was trying to look fierce and proud, Sara thought, but his face reflected a bitter cunning. "You'll be sorry you said that, Gabriel. You'll all be sorry — each of you bastards." His sour look took in the men one by one. "You think you can buy my son with your money and your pool table, but I'll get him back."

They stood in disgusted silence while the man slammed into his truck, backed crazily down the ramp, turned, and raced out to the highway. "I trust that's all just talk," said Ben.

"Who knows!" Gabe shrugged. "He is kind of crazy."

"Sara, you're shivering." Richard rushed her into the barn. "Hurry and put on some dry things. After you have some supper, you can fill us in on what really happened that upset you so."

Sara took a hot shower and pulled on pants and a sweater over long underwear. She looked at the blue dress. She could pick the burrs off, but in many places the material puckered where strands of the wool had been pulled; threads were broken, so the weave had holes in it. Dirt and wet moss had stained the skirt. Kyra might want to paint her in that dress, but Sara didn't ever want to put it on again. She rolled it into a bundle and took it to the common room.

She could hear the clatter of plates and murmur of voices coming from the kitchen, and, thinking everyone was there, she went to the wood stove and opened it up. She was about to throw in the dress when Richard came along and saw her. "Hey! Isn't that Kyra's dress?"

"It was. I've ruined it."

"Don't throw it on the fire. Burning wool makes a terrible stench."

"I'll put it in the trash."

"Wait a minute! I remember when Kyra bought that dress from the woman who wove the material. It was expensive."

"I know. I don't think it can be fixed." Reluctantly Sara spread the dress out on the chaise. The burrs and the dirt and the sad state of the material were plain to see. To her dismay, Kyra came in.

"There you are. I was just going to see if I could do anything for you besides keep your supper hot."

"Look at that dress," said Richard. "Sara was going to burn it up."

That startled Kyra. She looked at the dress and then at Sara. "I can see the dress is in bad shape. And I can see that Sara is too." Kyra pushed the dress aside and made Sara sit beside her on the chaise. "Did you want to get rid of the dress so it won't remind you about whatever happened to-day?"

"I can't bear to look at the dress again."

"That's too bad. Why don't you give it to Blanche to put away for a while. Maybe she can even fix it, and I do want to paint you in it." Kyra gave Sara a persuasive look and then glanced at Richard and laughed. "Oho! There went my Christmas surprise."

"It sounds like a nifty one." Richard took Sara's hand and pulled her to her feet. "Now, you'll fade away if you don't revive yourself with the entree of the day — Richard Brad-ford's famous split-pea soup. Followed by Blanche's superb chocolate marshmallow sponge cake. We made them to cele-brate your debut in the theater."

Her father's announcement was matter-of-fact, Sara thought. He intended neither irony nor sarcasm, yet he didn't seem to be aware of how it stung her when he mentioned the play. Perhaps Gabe hadn't told them what a disaster it had been. She followed them into the kitchen and slipped into the empty seat next to Gabe.

"Are you all right?" Gabe asked. "My father can be really weird sometimes — the way he talks. The way he drives. Well — you saw — "

Sara looked at him in surprise. Here she was full of agony over the play, and he was worried about what might have hap-pened when she was with his father. "I'm not *that* all right. But it's nothing to do with your father."

"You gave us a terrible scare, Sara," Harvey said sternly. "When you didn't arrive on the late bus, we were extremely concerned."

"Indeed we were," Blanche told her. "I phoned your friend Margaret. She said you'd taken your coat out of the locker and gone home, but no one had seen you after the play. We didn't know what could have happened to you."

"Especially when I would have seen you from the bus if you'd been walking along the road," said Gabe.

"Did you hide in the woods?" Demetri asked.

"I didn't hide. I didn't want to talk to anyone. And I was walking home. After a while the path disappeared and all I could do was keep walking north — I hoped — toward the barn. Then when I came to a brook I followed it and it came out by the road. That was lucky. It took me a long time, though, and I'm really tired."

"Were you scared?" Demetri asked.

"Sure. I was scared I was lost. I was scared of Mr. Courbeau. He was drunk and he drove like a wild man. But those weren't the worst things."

"What could be worse!" Gabe was still concerned over his father's behavior.

"Being laughed at in front of the whole school."

"Why is that worse than being lost in the woods?" asked Zeke. As a guide, he knew what could happen when people panicked in the woods: they could be severely injured; they could even die.

"Or being frightened in a car with a drunk!" exclaimed Blanche.

"Being laughed at was awful." The misery of the experience surged up again inside her. "It was so — *public*. And before the assembly I couldn't get the kids to work together when I was responsible for our group. It was a mess and everyone saw it and Worthington was disgusted and Cherylene fainted — "

"Your priorities are mixed up," Zeke said. "You're upset about the wrong things. Where you had control of the situation, you were great. You should be proud of yourself that you didn't panic in the woods — that you worked your way out by keeping your head."

"You really think so?" Sara was amazed.

"I do."

"And I'm proud of you for keeping your head," said her father, "and not letting that stinker Courbeau — sorry, Gabe — panic you either."

"You do have guts!" Ben announced.

Sara had never expected to be praised in such frank words nor did she suspect how relieved such praise would make her feel. She didn't mind too much when Richard lectured her. "You should put the rest of the day in perspective, Sara. When other people don't work with you, it's everybody's problem, not yours alone. As for your teacher — your Mr. Unworthyton there, he should have checked things out and known that your group was in trouble."

"He didn't even believe me when I tried to tell him." Sara liked the idea of his being called Unworthyton.

"Then it's his problem too," Richard went on. "He doesn't sound like the most experienced teacher around."

"I don't know why you feel so awful about it," Gabe said. "I heard a lot of kids say it was the best assembly they'd ever seen."

163

"Didn't it occur to you," Richard asked, "that they weren't laughing *at you*? That what was going on, whether you all meant it to be or not, struck people as funny?"

"I couldn't see it that way. Not then."

"But you could now."

"I'll try."

"Great." Richard was in a philosophical mood. "You know, you think of what happens to a piece of pottery — that out of earth and fire come its beauty and strength. I could be very poetic here — and carry on about shaping something, a pot or your life, out of the grit and soil of earth. And how, without the torture of the flame, you'd have nothing permanent. Nothing that would last. How the grit and the hurt put the shape and the character into that pot — or your life. What I'm trying to tell you is that even when some things hurt terribly, if you live through them, there'll be a strength and a shape that never could have been there before. Will you try to remember that?"

"I'll remember," Sara promised.

# 13

"Will you pose for me this morning?" Kyra stood in the doorway of Sara's bedroom.

Sara was cocooned into a sleeping bag overlaid with a Hud-
son's Bay blanket. She yawned and tried to wake up. "You
want to start today?"

"It will take a good many hours to paint the kind of portrait I want to do — in oils — and Christmas isn't that far
away."

"Right." Sara tried to sit up without unzipping the bag.
Their unheated bedrooms had taken on an Arctic tinge, and
she could see the vapor wafting up from her lips as she spoke.
She had placed her long underwear, pants, shirt, and sweater
where she could grab them and run to dress in the bathroom,
which had a small electric heater.

When Sara wiggled she dislodged Fonzie, who flowed out
from under the blanket in an arching stretch, strolled to the
pile of clothing, and after stepping haughtily about on the
fuzzy sweater, lay down on it, as if he dared Sara to abandon
him to the cold, bare floor.

"Was Blanche able to rescue the blue dress?" asked Kyra.

"All she could do was cut off the bottom and rehem it. It's

a tunic now. I'm sorry I tried to burn it up. That was dumb, you know."

"I know, but maybe you'll wear it more often as a top. Anyway, do put it on. With some jeans. Now let's let some light in here." Kyra pulled the curtains at the east window, and a spear of sunlight flashed through to strike at Fonzie and kindle brown-gold depths in his eyes that Sara had never seen before.

"That cat has tiger eyes!" exclaimed Kyra. "You know — that semiprecious stone they call a tiger eye that has a hidden glow in it? I wonder if I could paint it —"

She stared thoughtfully at Fonzie, and then her eyes studied the rest of the room — the light from the window and how it fell on the floor, on the chair, on the shelves. "What is that?"

"What?" Sara had unzipped the bag and was gathering courage for her plunge into the frigid room.

"That cat on the shelf —"

"It's a china cat. Porcelain, I guess. It was part of my father's ceramic collection, and it was one of a pair."

"Could it be Staffordshire? I know the Staffordshire dogs are famous. But I didn't know they ever made cats. They could be collectors' items."

"Maybe it was a rare pair and that's why Richard was so upset when I broke one. He went into a rage. He was going to hit me. I had nightmares about it for years — seeing this ogre he'd turned into rising up in front of me with a raised fist. That's why I was so terrified when Fonzie broke the punch bowl. It was like breaking the china cat and having a nightmare all at the same time."

"I remember how scared you were, and I didn't understand why. Did Richard really hit you?"

"That's what I don't remember. I always see him and the"

ogre as they're about to do it, but I can't remember what happened next. It's as if my mind blocked it out."

"Now that you're older and you know Richard better, do you still have the nightmare?"

"Only once since I've been here. After Demetri fell down the gravel pit and cut his cheek —"

"And you felt responsible for it."

"Yes."

"Aha! I've made up my mind. I can see the whole painting. Bring Fonzie and bring that porcelain cat —"

"But Richard hates cats! He'll hate the picture if you put them in."

"I don't think he will. Richard isn't a hater. He has a flaming temper, but once he's burned it out, it doesn't leave any residue. Trust me, Sara. You know I like to do paintings that make people see things in a new way!"

Sara thought about it. She could sense Kyra's enthusiasm for the symbolism as well as the composition and the color, yet she felt very uneasy about agreeing to it. "Couldn't you paint just Fonzie and me? Richard's finally used to having Fonzie around. He even stopped to admire his shape once before he threw him off the pool table."

"I'll put you and Fonzie in the foreground. And quite innocently, in the shadowy background, I will paint in the Staffordshire cat. You'll see. It will be an exorcism. The end of your nightmares."

So Sara posed, and Fonzie, glad of the attention and the warmth of the studio, posed too, his purr sometimes being the only sound in the stilled atmosphere of intense concentration. The studio was one of the few heated areas in the barn, along with the shops, the common room, and the kitchen — all oases of warmth. People rushed through the frigid areas in between with the determination of explorers trying to reach the Pole and get home.

By Thanksgiving Day, on which they had what Richard called a feast of noble proportions, winter surrounded the barn, not with snow, but with plunging temperatures that turned puddles and nearby ponds into steel-sheened mirrors. When Gabe let the goats out briefly each day, their hoofs striking the iron-hard earth made as much noise as their bells, and with the ground frozen down at least a foot, Zeke turned to the cold storage rooms to supply the cooks with turnips and winter squashes, carrots and potatoes.

As Christmas drew near, they were all busy. Workshop doors, closed now to treasure the heat, sometimes bore emphatic signs: KEEP OUT.

Sara heard Demetri wail, "I can't stay anywhere but the bathroom and the kitchen."

"And not so long in the bathroom," Blanche told him. "Yesterday you were in the upstairs bathroom with your building blocks, making castles, for hours."

"You could have come in."

"Yes, I could have. But I like my privacy."

"Demetri!" Kyra scolded. "The bathroom is not the place to play. You bring your blocks downstairs and play here."

"You read in the bathroom."

"Sometimes. Briefly."

"The other day you —"

"Enough! We have to think about other people. We have to share and we have to be fair."

"I want my own house. I want to play out where it's warm.

I want to go swimming!" Demetri worked up to what Blanche called "a real touse."

Kyra sighed and gave him one sharp smack on the bottom, which he barely felt as he was so well padded with clothing. "That's for keeping on at it when I asked you to stop." Then she gave him a ferocious hug and a lot of kisses. "And those are for reminding me what it's like to want something when you can't have it. Like playing out in the sunshine and swimming. I'd like that too."

"We'll take you skating, Demi," Sara promised. "If we can find you some skates."

Actually Sara wanted Gabe to take her skating. He had slipped into a shed at the Courbeaus' early one morning and brought back his hockey skates and borrowed a pair Vonnie had outgrown that were still too big for Elise. They fit Sara, but so tightly that she could only use her thinnest socks with them.

"That's good," Gabe tried to tell her. "Pro hockey players wear skates that fit like gloves. No lumpy socks to mess up their feet."

"Don't their feet freeze?"

"They don't stay still long enough."

Zeke found a pair of small skates in a secondhand store and bought them for Demetri. On a Sunday afternoon, Zeke drove Sara and Gabe and Demetri to Martin's Corners Lake, which was really a series of small ponds linked by marshes where channels of clear ice were dotted with hummocks of frozen grass. The good skaters liked to race the channels, trying to jump the hummocks, or to join the boisterous hockey games whose players took over each of the ponds. Skaters who wanted only to glide, or attempt an occasional fancy figure, had to watch out for flailing hockey sticks, flying pucks, and hurtling players, as well as tripping tufts of weedy sedge. Sara's dream of skating hand in hand with Gabe, of gracefully gliding over crystal ice under a spotlight of sun while everyone turned to admire them, was dashed as Gabe spurted off to find a place in one of the games. Zeke had brought his skates and stick too and rushed off, leaving Sara, who had only skated once before on an indoor rink, to help Demetri.

For the first fifteen minutes Demetri thought it was fun. He didn't mind falling. He slid, belly-down on the ice, and announced, "I'm a turtle." He let Sara haul him to his feet, and together they attempted to skate. Sara bent over to take Demetri's hand and tried to skate from a slight crouch that kept sending her off balance. Demetri's glide was shorter than hers. It was like playing Red Light handicapped by taking only Baby Steps. They swooped and they stumbled; they clashed and they fell, over and over. Sara wore less padding, and before long she felt as bruised as a supermarket peach. In half an hour, Demetri rebelled. His mittens were wet through and his reddened fingers ached. He lay on the ice and refused to arise. "Take my skates off."

"I can't take your skates off here. Your shoes are back at the head of the lake."

"I can walk."

"In your stocking feet?"

"Carry me."

"You know I can't do that when I'm on skates! Now get up. Let's go back to the truck. I'm cold too."

"No." He closed his eyes, shutting out the dazzle of sunlight striking the ice, shutting out the furious expression on

Sara's face as she loomed over him. Tears rolled from under his eyelids. Sara was sure they would freeze on his cheeks. She stood there, so cold — with only thin socks and thin leather encasing her feet and ankles — that the blades of her skates seemed like knives slicing into the soles of her feet. She was ready to cry too, especially when Demetri went limp and refused to help when she attempted to pull him up. The joy of skating was a delusion.

She decided that Demetri was as stubborn as his mother, who continued to paint the cats into the portrait despite her foreboding and who, as she painted, talked more and more about returning to Crete to be warm — glowingly, radiantly warm inside and out! Sara had hoped the sittings would bring them closer together and then that the presentation of the portrait to Richard at Christmas would suddenly carry them all into what she still dreamed of as the magic of a family circle. Instead she felt Kyra putting more distance between them and not trying to understand Sara and how she felt.

"All right," said Sara to Demetri, "lie there. I'm through with you!" Nobody cares, she thought. Nobody ever wants to do anything to help anybody else. She started to skate away, but her numb feet betrayed her. She couldn't control them, and she fell heavily onto her knees. She leaned forward, rested her head on the ice, and pounded her fists on its impassive surface. Her father probably would have intoned, "Woe! Woe is me!" Sara flatly said, "Damn. Damn. Damn."

Then she heard two familiar sounds. One was the snickety-wheeze, almost like a stifled sneeze, of a camera resetting itself on automatic wind. The other was Richard's laugh. It was too much. She stretched out flat on the ice and burst into tears.

"Oh my Currier and Ives! What ever happened to good old-fashioned skating parties!" Richard's skates flashed, the blades shushing out a tiny ice storm as he stopped short, inches from her nose. The indignity of her being there flat on the ice — his assurance he could stop at that precise spot — without slashing into her face — overwhelmed her. She did not know which to do first — scream with rage or bellow with frustration. So she rolled into a sitting position and sat, ominously quiet. Kyra, shuffling about in the padded snowmobile boots she'd bought to keep her feet warm in the barn, took another picture of Sara.

"Don't!" Sara screamed. "Don't take my picture. Go away and leave me alone! All of you!"

"It must be the Ice Follies!" Richard went on, trying to humor her out of it. "Or are you really hurt somewhere?"

"Yes. I'm hurt."

"Ankle? Arm? Head?"

"Inside!" Sara wept. "Inside."

Her father was alarmed. "Then we'd better get you home. Or over to the clinic."

"Oh, I give up." Sara pushed herself off the ice in disgust. "I haven't broken anything. Except my feelings and they're all tangled up."

"Then come and skate with me. That's what I came for. Kyra and I decided we couldn't let you kids have all the fun —"

Fun! Sara glared at her father. He was smiling eagerly, inviting her to partake of the day's offerings — the cheering sun, the ice, the joy of swooping about with exhilarating strokes. He held his hands out. "I came to skate with you. Old Shuffle-Boot there won't even try."

"Watch it!" Kyra teased. "Old Shuffle-Boot can take telling pictures for sheer revenge."

Demetri sat up. "Skate with me, Richard."

"Later," Richard said. "Saradipity? Ready?"

She nodded, and he showed her how to cross hands; his grip was steadying. "Are you left-footed or right-footed?"

"I don't know."

"If you take after me, you're left-footed, so we'll start left. One, two, three — we're off —"

Her first strokes were short and tentative, but soon Richard's strong pace caught her up. She matched her stride to his and leaned into the curves as they eluded spikes of grass and rough patches of ice. Richard loosened his hold once to wave, and Sara saw Zeke salute with his hockey stick. They swerved around the players' ice, past their makeshift goal of chicken-wire and lath, and wove in and out of the path of other skaters in the channels. When Sara saw the cars and trucks parked at the head of the lake, she didn't want to stop.

"Are you going back for Demetri?"

"I promised, didn't I?"

"You did."

"Had enough? Or do you want to skate back with me?"

"I'll skate. I'll fly! I'll glide! I'll swoon with rapture!" She tried to speak her father's language. He encouraged her with a grin. As they glissaded past the first group of hockey players, she saw Gabe, and this time she waved.

"That's my girl!" said Richard. "You'll be in the Ice Follies yet!"

When he left her to help Demetri, she kept on skating, still feeling his pace and his stance, following the rhythm he'd set.

It worked. She didn't fall. There was a joy in skating. She'd discovered it and it swept her along.

Before she left the lake with her father and Kyra and Demetri, she turned to watch Gabe, who had shouted that he'd finish his game and return with Zeke. All the boys seemed to be unconscious of the fact that they were on skates, except when they were pushing for distance, furiously stroking into a long, swooping glide. They ran on their blades, hopped on them, jumped on them, and did the most extraordinary split-second about-faces on them. They all seemed to have the nimble sure-footedness of dancers, and among them, Gabe's figure stood out as his body flowed in easy lines, from the tilt of his head through the swing of his arms and the curve of his torso. The next time they came to skate, Sara hoped she'd be able to skate with him, just as she had with her father. If she could keep Gabe away from the hockey games long enough!

The week before Christmas Ben and Zeke brought in a gigantic tree and set it up in the common room. They all helped to decorate it with anything that inspired them: brilliant yarn Eyes of God made by Blanche; crisp origami birds made by Sara; popcorn garlands hungrily put together by Gabe and Demetri; silvered pine cones prepared by Zeke; thin ceramic shapes of stars and moons, rolled out and cut with cookie cutters and fired with a shiny white-and-gold glaze by Richard; figures of animals jigsawed by Harvey and painted with imaginative designs by Kyra; and four strings of colored fairy lights that Richard insisted were needed to make the tree sparkle and twinkle and look full of delight. "You don't want a glum Christmas tree glowering at you, all dark and broody. It's got to have shimmer — "

Shimmer it did, and Sara had seldom been happier than on

the Christmas Eve they spent together, close to the tree whose forest scent was roused by the warmth from the stove. Richard read *A Child's Christmas in Wales,* his rich voice reembroidering the already flowing text with piquant cheer and dramatic depth. Zeke bought new strings for his guitar and managed it tunefully enough to accompany the singing of carols; and in the morning, before they made yet another feast of noble proportions, they exchanged presents — the homemade items that had been prepared in gleeful secret. Except for Blanche's afghans, which had progressed steadily for all to see during the autumn weeks as she sat on her chaise.

Kyra and Sara watched — Kyra with anticipation, Sara with apprehension — as Richard unwrapped the portrait. He pulled the tissue off with a flourish and propped the canvas on a chair by a window.

"That's a stunning frame," he said, admiring the scrolled frame of cherry, which had been rubbed to bring out the grain. "Did you make it, Zeke? I see your name on this tag too!"

"Glad you like it. It had to be special to frame a painting like that."

"Indeed!" Richard studied the painting. The style was realistic, very different from the abstract shapes Kyra used in her landscapes, or "inscapes," as she had begun to call them. It was a medium-sized canvas, but the figure was not a life-sized head and shoulders like most conventional portraits. It was rather a study of the torso of a young girl — obviously Sara — wearing a blue blouse and jeans, sitting in a wooden chair, with light from a window at one side of the picture illuminating her features and her reddish curls. It fell also onto the orange-furred cat she held in her lap, a cat whose eyes looked directly out from the canvas, seeming to challenge the viewer, giving the impression that there was intense energy vibrating behind those glowing eyes and that at a single sound the cat would rouse and leap away, leaving the girl with her hand curved over an empty space. Behind the girl's shoulder, rising up from a shelf in the background, was a china cat whose white body could not be completely lost in the shadows, for its shape was still dimly defined by the light from the window in the painting. Its opaque eyes stared darkly, again at the viewer. The contrast of the direct gaze of the cats to the downward contemplative cast of the girl's eyes was strangely disquieting.

Sara knew the likeness to her appearance was true — the carefully limned features, the right proportions, the subtle tonal values to her skin and hair — and she guessed that Kyra had caught her attitude. Something that she could not come out and say about herself. Perhaps Kyra had caught both her dreams and her defenses. Yet she was uncomfortably sure that Kyra had overplayed it by including the two cats.

Richard was shaking his head. "By God, you've got Sara to a dipity. Perfect, Kyra. That angle of her head, that wondering look she has. And, of course, the mere details like the nose and mouth and the eyes — they're absolutely true. I'd like it a little better — not a criticism of the painting, mind you, be- cause you must have done it for the composition — but I'd personally relate to it just a mite more if Sara's eyes weren't so hidden. If there was eye contact, as they say. This makes me want to say. 'Look up. Look at me, Sara,' and then we'd have a good long look at each other."

Kyra threw a piece of red-and-gold wrapping paper and a handful of ribbons up in the air. Sara thought she looked triumphant, yet all she said was, "I'm glad you think it's a good likeness. It wasn't an easy painting to do."

Richard seemed puzzled. "I suppose it is hard to tackle such a direct style, especially after your imaginative land-scapes."

"This took some imaginative insight too, and a lot of help from Sara."

"I think it's beautiful," said Blanche. "Although you didn't use much color. Of course there's some bright blue and orange and some golds and a few reddish places —"

"No greens and purples and pinks?" Kyra laughed. "Oh, Blanchie! I do love you!" She embraced her, burying her face in Blanche's soft, wrinkly neck, hugging her hard. "I'll paint you a picture with all the colors you can name in it. Just like one of your heavenly afghans."

"You do that, dear, and Harvey and I will treasure it. Where are you going to hang this picture, Richard? Here in this room where we can all admire it?"

"Yes. If you'd like that. I'll just leave it here for now." He set it on the floor, braced against the wall, and stepped back to look at it again. "Sara, why is that cat — I don't mean Fonzie — so familiar? I know it's a Staffordshire cat. Quite rare. I had a pair of them years ago, and with all the moving around we did, I suppose they were broken or lost somewhere. Do you remember them?"

"Haven't you noticed the one on the shelf in my room? It's the one Kyra used in the painting."

"I haven't exactly been a prowling parent, checking out your room. How did you come by it?"

"Gran gave it to me. She found it rolled up in a dress of

Mother's in the trunk you sent back from India. Gran said I ought to have something of Mother's to keep, and that was the only thing there was. She gave the clothes away."

Richard sat down. He picked up a long piece of blue ribbon from the floor and began methodically untwisting it and rolling it up.

"Of course it's really your cat," said Sara. "Mother was just the caretaker for your ceramic collection."

"She was a fine curator. The best. There are two boxes at the back of the pottery full of rare ceramics that she packed and unpacked for me many times. I don't know why she had separated the cat from the rest of the pieces. Maybe because there was only one. I wonder what happened to the other."

"Don't you remember?" Sara asked, unbelieving. "You really don't remember!" She kept on staring at her father. All those years of nightmare about what to her was catastrophic, and the incident had not even left a fragment in his mind! She kept on staring at him in amazement.

"From the look on your face, you must have broken one of them!" Richard exclaimed. "By God, did you?"

"Yes, I did. I've never forgotten it because you were so upset. I thought — I really thought — you were going to strike me."

"Oh God!" Richard thrust his legs out straight before him and let his arms flop limply over the sides of his chair. "What a monster I must have seemed to you — to make you remember it all this time. Now you remind me, I do dimly recall it. We were staying in Stoke-on-Trent. I don't know why I was so intrigued with those nasty cats. They are ugly, and I've never been fond of live cats either. Look, Sara, I give you leave to break this one any time you want."

178

Sara nodded. She felt unstable, as if she were buffeted by a sudden gust of wind as she stood at the edge of a cliff.

"Well, here I am," Richard carried on. "Exposed to one and all as a lurid, ill-tempered father —" He let the words fall into the quiet room, waiting for someone to pick them up, clean them off, and hand them back transformed.

Gabe did. "No you're not!" he protested. "I know what a mean, ill-tempered father is like. You could never be like that!"

"And did I strike you for breaking the cat?" Richard asked Sara.

"I don't know. I thought you were going to and I can't remember if you did."

"Can you forgive me? For a bad memory that's haunted you all these years?" Richard asked. He sat up expectantly, and she felt he was willing her to say yes. Yet she felt he wanted something more than just her approval. He was looking deeply into her eyes, seeking her out as he had sought the girl in the portrait who had baffled him. He was seeing Sara as a person and listening to her. And because he was listening, she could say, "Yes. I'll forgive you and I'll give you the cat. For your collection."

"Fair enough! And Kyra, you are a mysterious, clairvoyant, brilliantly talented schemer! A portrait of my daughter, indeed. Do you have a name for it? Is it *Girl with Felines?* or *The Potter's Daughter?* or just *Sara Bradford?*"

Kyra went over and kissed the tip of Richard's nose. "It's called *Portrait of a Dreamer.*"

# 14

"Can we leave the tree up until after New Year's Eve?" Sara asked. "I'll miss it when we take it down. It's almost like another person in the room."

"You feel it has a *presence*, eh? Then we'll keep it until Twelfth Night," Richard decreed. "That's the old tradition anyway. You make an evening of it and have a huge bowl of syllabub or some such, and play games and tell stories and take the ornaments off one by one and pack them away. And then — out goes the tree — to be another ghost of Christmas past."

Zeke fingered one of the branches. "The needles haven't dried out too much. If you keep it watered, Sara — fill up that crock it's standing in every day — it should be all right to keep it here for ten more days."

"I'll remember," Sara promised. "What are we going to do to celebrate New Years' Eve?"

"Would you like a party for your friends?" Kyra asked.

"A reunion of the *dramatis personae* of the great castle debacle?" Richard suggested.

"Hardly!" Sara gave her father a disgusted look.

"Why ever not? The greatest reunions are usually those of people who survived disasters together."

Sara wasn't quite ready to laugh off the experience yet, but she was beginning to understand her father better and not to let his offhand remarks bother her as much. "I'd like a party of just us."

"I'd like a really special time together too," Kyra said. "Because I might as well tell you now, I'm planning to go home. Back to Crete. I told Richard last night."

Sara looked at her father and saw how tired he was. His eyes seemed narrowed — squinchy, Gran would have said — as if he hadn't slept much the night before. He had been extraordinarily quiet, Sara realized, at the supper table. She had put it down to everyone's recuperating from the festivities of the previous day.

"You can't!" Sara faced Kyra. "You can't go! I don't want you to. Richard, you can't let her and Demi go!"

"Those were my very words —" her father said.

"Why?" asked Sara. "Don't you like it here? Don't you love us — I mean, love Richard, anymore?"

Kyra clasped her hands in front of her, as if she could grasp a convincing answer out of the air for them. Blanche sat down with a thud on her chaise. Zeke kept on tugging at a branch of the tree. Harvey tamped tobacco into his pipe so tightly it would probably never light. Ben turned away and picked up a newspaper, apparently feeling this was more of a private crisis than a group discussion. Gabe, who had been practicing trick shots, put down the cuestick and walked over to lean on the back of the couch where Sara sat. Demetri lay on his back on the floor near the stove, holding a toy airplane over his head and humming as he looped it about through the air.

"That's the problem. I do love you all. Very much. And especially Richard and you, Sara. I can feel myself settling into the group life and being carried along by it without any initiative on my part, and that's what I'm not ready for. I'm not ready to give up my independence. I'd be tugging at the web, folks, in another week or two. Being ornery. Plucking at the threads. Breaking patterns. Dislodging affections. No. It's time for me to go." She tried to lighten the mood her announcement had created. "Besides, my tan has faded. So has Demetri's. We've got to go lie on a beach and get brown and warm again."

"You could go to Florida — and come back," Gabe offered. Sara was surprised. At first she thought he was speaking up for Richard, wanting things to be right for the man who had become his teacher, his big brother, his father substitute. Then she saw he was speaking for himself. "I thought you were going to teach me about photography. I've been saving up to buy a camera."

"I'm sorry about that. We could have had a lot of fun —"

"We'll fix up the darkroom you've been wanting," Gabe beseeched her. "We can build the partitions and benches this weekend, and Zeke could start scrounging for the plumbing stuff. How about that? Ben? Zeke?"

Ben lowered his newspaper. "I'd be glad to do that, Kyra. That's the kind of bribery I enjoy."

"Oh, please!" Kyra covered her face with her hands for a moment, as if she could shove the tears in her eyes back out of sight. "Don't you see? You're all doing it. Tightening those helpful, loving strands. Somehow it was easier to split up with

Georgios than it is to walk away from all of you. It's been a very hard decision to make —"

"Does it have to be a permanent decision?" Zeke asked. "I was going to tell you after New Year's that I'm planning to leave for a while. I'm a restless guy and I need a change. Down South or out West. Wherever I can find odd jobs. But only until it's gardening time in New Hampshire. I'll be back with the spring birds. Kyra, if you only need to recoat your tan and claim your right to be a free agent, why don't you hack around the warm parts of the States for a while and come back in the spring?"

"It's not a change of scene I need. It's needing to be sure of who I am. You see, Richard came along as I was only beginning to find out. And he's so outgoing, so all-embracing, so persuasive, that I let him take over. He just kind of directed my life, my painting. Even Demi. It was right for Richard when he inherited this barn to fix it up and find such a wonderful group of talented friends to share it. When he wrote to persuade me to come, he said I'd love it. And I do. But I can't stay." Sara interpreted the expression on her face and the firmness in her voice to mean she was both sad and determined. "I have too much unfinished business with myself. With my painting. And with Demetri. Sometimes I feel as if I'm letting him be brought up by committee. And then —" she looked at them with glistening eyes — "I wonder how I dare try to bring him up without you. But I have to try."

Sara wanted Richard to say something, but he didn't. He seemed to have withdrawn and, in a tense, dour way, refused to be part of the argument. Probably he'd given Kyra all his arguments, tried all his charm and gentle persuasions last night. Having failed he had nothing more to say. The sundew was in shadow; its outer leaves were sere and dusty; the sparkle was gone.

Abruptly Kyra got up and made Demetri move out of the way so she could throw some chunks of wood into the stove. "Who wants a game of Ping-Pong?" she asked. "Or pool? Or Dictionary — so we all can play?"

"Not me." Richard left the room. Sara listened, wondering if he would go up the stairs to bed or down the stairs to the pottery. She wondered if Kyra would rush after him, and when she didn't Sara wondered if she should try to console her father. She suspected he was feeling as frustrated, as unhappy, perhaps even as empty inside, as she had felt at various times in various places, and she could share his sense of loss at that very moment. It was the end of her dream that Kyra and Richard would marry and Demetri and Sara would be their family and they would all live happily ever after.

She remembered her father's restlessness. Without Kyra's steadying influence, would he become bored with being a successful potter? If people drifted away from the group in the barn, would he give it up and drift off too? And what would happen to her? Would she have to tag around the world after him again? The lights on the Christmas tree blurred and then ran together through her tears.

"Oh, horrors!" Kyra faced them. "I have certainly put my foot right through the Christmas cheer. Richard opting out. Sara in tears. For God's sake, somebody take me on at Ping-Pong and let me keep up my fighting spirit."

"You're on," Zeke said. "Doubles, any of you? Sara? Gabe? Ben?"

Ben shook his head and kept on reading the newspaper.

Sara sat staring at her hands in her lap until Gabe leaned over the back of the couch and asked, "Do you want to play pool?" just as Blanche asked her, "Would you like a game of cribbage?"

"Don't treat me as if I was a little kid!" Sara snapped. "Playing games isn't going to help."

Gabe pulled away, and Sara was instantly sorry. She knew he wanted to make her feel better and so did Blanche. "I'll go make tea. Would any of you like some tea?"

Gabe had gone back to practice pool shots and didn't answer. The Ping-Pong players were spanking the ball back and forth with vicious energy. Blanche said, "A cup would taste good. Thank you, Sara dearie."

Harvey followed her into the kitchen. "How about some spiced cinnamon tea?"

"Why not?" Sara turned on the faucet to fill the kettle so hard that the water poured over the outside of it. She shook it and drops flew from it in all directions. Harvey took it out of her hand, wiped it dry with a towel, set it on the stove, and eased Sara into a seat at the table. "Put a wet kettle on that stove and you'll make a rust spot. That would make Blanchie unhappy. But not as unhappy as you are. You want to talk about it? Or let it simmer?"

"Talking's not going to change Kyra's mind. Or make my father take it any better. He's used to having everything go the way he wants it to."

"Letting it simmer won't help either."

"What I want," Sara burst out, "is to have a father and a mother — and a brother like Demi — to live in one place long enough to get through school without moving! I want to know what it feels like to be part of that kind of family. I thought there was really a good chance it would happen, and it's all sliding away and I can't stop it."

"Families change, just like individuals. Sometimes new babies arrive. Brothers and sisters grow up and move out. Parents split up and sometimes they each marry someone else. They start new families as easily as TV series start spin-offs. Or one parent dies. Or kids run away and disappear. Stamping a related group of people *family* doesn't guarantee a thing, Sara. Not anymore." Harvey gave a long sigh. "I grew up on a farm in Vermont, with five brothers and two sisters and both my parents and my four grandparents living to ripe old ages and three aunts and four uncles and thirty-two first cousins all living in the same county. People believed in God and family. You knew God was watching you, and you also knew fifty-two pairs of family eyes and ears knew everything about you. I'll bet a lot of my brothers and sisters and cousins wanted to move to unwatched territory as quickly as I did. Kyra has several points, you see. You can't always live the way other people expect you to live, and other people in your life can never solve things for you, until you know who you are or what you want."

"Maybe," said Sara. "But if you had a family, then wouldn't it be easier to find out about yourself?"

"Who came first! The chicken or the egg!" Harvey exclaimed. "Let's take care of an immediate problem. Where are the cinnamon sticks? You hunt for them while I put these cloves in the lemon slices."

Sara carried the tray of mugs, steaming with spicy tea, into the common room. She passed them out and then sat down to sip at hers. Not even the shimmer on the Christmas tree could lighten her spirit.

Kyra's announcement spoiled everyone's holiday feelings as they approached the New Year. They became uncomfortable with each other and with themselves; things went unsaid that should have been said. Burnt toast in the morning became insult instead of accident; mealtimes, which before had been full of anecdotes and jokes and earnest discussions, were passed in polite meaningless conversation, full of pauses. Richard tried to persuade Kyra to go to Boston with him over New Year's, partly to deliver the canvases she wanted to sell through a gallery and partly to see if a "time-out" for the two of them would change her mind. He phoned every hotel he could think of, but couldn't get a room reservation. Then he retreated to the pottery and tried to take his frustrations out on the clay. He wedged and wedged and he threw enormous tall pots and then broke them down and tossed the clay into the slop barrel. Sara spent some time in the pottery with him, shaping a bowl from coils, just in case he wanted to talk, and she found his silence frightening, because the quiet was so different from his usual torrent of words and ideas or out-pouring of song. She wondered if he even knew she was there.

Nor did Kyra's wish that they all spend a special New Year's Eve together happen. Two days before, Zeke hauled out his backpack and duffel bag and spent the morning organizing his things. By noon he was ready to leave. "I'm leaving before we have a snowstorm and transportation is fouled up along the coast. If I catch a Greyhound tonight, I could even celebrate the New Year under a palm tree. That reminds me — how's your Tahiti trip coming, Harvey? Air fares are going up all the time. You better pick a date and buy your tickets as soon as you can."

"I'm still thinking about it," Harvey said.

"Good for you." Zeke kissed Blanche goodbye. "When the Canada geese come through next March, you'll know I won't be far behind. Harve, Richard, Gabe — take care. Sara, stay out of the funny papers." He gave her a hug and a smack on the forehead and a poke in the ribs, all at the same time. "Kyra, Demi, when do you leave?"

"On January fifth. The day before the Christmas tree comes down. The day before Twelfth Night."

"I wonder if there's a Thirteenth Night," said Richard, but his heart was not in the query.

Zeke had Kyra in his arms, kissing her goodbye. "What can I say? Goodbye? Au revoir? Auf Wiedersehen? I'll be seeing you?"

"Make it I'll-be-seeing-you and come to Crete."

"If I can do it by raft or by freighter — el cheapo — I might make it sometime."

Ben appeared with an overnight bag. "I'm going to drive Zeke to New York. He can take the bus from there. I have a sudden urge to stand in Times Square in the midst of a mob of people. Then I'll be content to do without mobs of people for another whole year."

By seven o'clock on New Year's Eve, Sara wished she'd invited some of the kids to come over. The barn was too silent, too shadowy, too echoing. Even though the Christmas tree still filled up part of the common room, and they turned its lights on, they deserted it to spend the evening around the kitchen table. Richard and Kyra were determined that they would play games and have fun together.

Richard made mulled wine, kept hot on the stove, and allowed Gabe and Sara to have some. Kyra had spent the afternoon making Greek *pita* to serve at midnight — little pastries with squash or spinach or meat filling. In one of them she hid a shiny dime, a symbol of good luck in the coming year for the finder. They played Dictionary, Crazy Eights, I Doubt It, and Hearts. They laughed and they teased and they talked, yet the laughter was often forced, the teasing sometimes had an edge to it, and the talk was insignificant. By eleven Sara had a headache from the wine. Demetri had wrapped himself in a blanket and fallen asleep on the floor.

At eleven Blanche said, "I'm sorry but I can't make it to midnight. I'll wish you a Happy New Year right now and I'm going to bed."

"I'm with you, Blanche." Harvey helped her up. "I'll pick out my *pita* and eat it for breakfast. Save me — that one. If the dime's in it, the luck will be as good in the morning. Happy New Year, my dears." He kissed Sara's and Kyra's hands in a mock courtly way. "And may the New Year be kind to us all."

"I'll take Demi upstairs," Kyra decided. "He wanted me to wake him at midnight, but he's so sound asleep I know he'll only be bewildered and cranky and cry."

"I'll carry him." Richard picked him up. "We'll be down to toast the New Year with you, though, so stay awake, kids."

Sara wondered if Gabe was as weary-eyed and heavy-hearted as she was. She remembered last New Year's Eve in Yellow Creek, spent at a party in Bethy-Sue's house. The girls had giggled on one side of the parlor, and the boys had hesitated on the other. Counting down to midnight and yelling "Happy New Year" and screeching out the words to "Auld Lang

Syne," and a few of the bolder ones exchanging kisses, had seemed exciting, tremblingly on the edge of not just a new year, but new experiences and new emotions.

"Let's put on the TV," said Sara. "I think they show Times Square. Maybe we'll see Ben."

She took the tray of *pita*. Gabe filled their mugs with more wine, and they moved into the common room. She perched on Blanche's chaise. Gabe stretched out on the couch. The only lights were the flares of the fairy bulbs and the reflections they cast from shiny ornaments on the tree and the bright rectangle of the TV tube. The only sound was the announcer, overenthusiastically describing what the eye could see — a mass of tiny, tiny people, heads all turned toward the spot above them where a ball outlined in blinking lights would descend at midnight.

"Do you suppose Ben's there, all alone in that crowd?" Sara asked.

"Maybe he's there. Maybe he's not alone — "

"Do you suppose Zeke's in Florida now?"

"Mmmm," murmured Gabe, setting his mug on the floor. Then his arm hung there, off the couch, motionless.

Sara asked quietly, "Gabe, are you asleep?"

He didn't answer.

The announcer's voice rose. "Here it comes, the moment we've been waiting for — the end of the old, worn-out year we've no more use for — and the start of a brand-new, let's-make-it-the-best-year-ever year ahead. Nine, eight — "

Sara sat solemnly on the chaise. The shrill pitch of the announcer's voice didn't penetrate Gabe's slumber. Sara wanted to shake him.

"Seven, six, five — "

And where were Kyra and Richard, who had insisted on observing New Year's Eve? Why hadn't they returned as they promised? Perhaps they were arguing. Perhaps they didn't know it was midnight. Perhaps, like Demetri, they had fallen asleep.

"— four, three, two, one. Hap–pee New Year!" A frenzy of horn-tooting and yelling rose up from the throng in Times Square while an orchestra throbbed the melody of "Auld Lang Syne."

"Happy New Year to me," Sara said softly. She took a sip of the mulled wine and, without looking, let her hand fall on a *pita*. The crust was tender, the filling sweet with squash. On the third bite her teeth closed on a hard object. She pulled it out, unwrapped the tiny square of wax paper, and there was the dime.

"So — Happy Lucky New Year to me." She put the dime in her jeans' pocket, covered Gabe with a crocheted afghan, turned off the tree lights and the TV, and went upstairs to bed. She didn't hear a sound as she passed the door to Kyra's and Richard's room. She was pleased to see Fonzie sleeping on her bed. She held him close and whispered in his ear, "Happy New Year. I wonder what this one will be like."

# 15

"Will you be here when we come home this afternoon?" Sara asked. She and Gabe were hustling into their parkas, getting ready to dash for the school bus, when Kyra came into the kitchen. She looked unexpectedly sophisticated in a trim wool sweater and tailored slacks.

"I'm afraid not. Richard checked the weather report. There's a chance of an overnight storm, so driving to Logan tomorrow might be difficult. It makes sense to head for Boston before it hits, and I'll be able to leave my paintings at the gallery this afternoon. I've made reservations at the airport hotel."

"Is Richard coming back tonight? Or is he staying to see you off?"

"I don't know. We're not good at farewells. Like right now. How can I say goodbye to you? The last few days have been hard for all of us, but we'll remember the good days, Demi and I. Especially since you came, Sara." Kyra put her hands on Sara's shoulders. "What a difference a few months here have made in you. She's changed, hasn't she, Gabe!"

"I guess so. I mean, she doesn't look much different but she does act different." Gabe gave Sara an approving glance that would have sent her spirits on a supersonic flight at another time.

"I think Sara does look different." Kyra studied her face. "You've got a gleam in your eye now, Sara. You're willing to try so many things you didn't dare before. And you'll conquer them. I can feel it. Trust yourself!"

Sara, in turn, studied Kyra. Already she felt a distance between them, not a sense of an ocean or their ages separating them, but a space in their experiences. It was a distance that Kyra, whose mind seemed to be as packed up and ready to leave as her baggage, imposed unknowingly. It made Sara sad.

She'd heard Kyra tell her to trust herself, and she felt that was what Kyra was trying to do by going away — to trust herself. If only they could both have trusted her father, perhaps things would have turned out differently. Things she wanted to tell Kyra, wishes stifled before she could utter them, rioted around in her head. It was too late.

Demetri ran in carrying the skates Zeke had given him. "You didn't pack these!"

"You won't need them. You won't have any ice to skate on in Crete."

"I want them. They're mine." He hugged the skates, even though the metal blades must have hurt as he pressed them tightly to his shirt. "Why are we going away? This is where I live!"

"Oh, Demi! Last week you couldn't wait to be where you could run out in the sun in your shorts and swim and play with your friends. You said you wanted to go home and you meant back to Crete."

"That's not what I want now."

"Oh, honey!" Kyra touched her son's hair lightly. "We

don't very often have what we want at the moment we want it. What puzzles me is do we ever know for sure when we have something we really want — before we let it go and make a terrible mistake?"

"Sara, come on. We'll miss the bus," Gabe warned. "Goodbye, Demi. Leave the skates here and maybe they'll grow a couple of sizes if you come back."

"What a lovely idea!" Kyra said, as Demetri handed the skates to Gabe. She kissed Gabe. "Thanks for being an older brother to Demi. Take care of yourself."

"You too!" Gabe plunged for the doorway.

Kyra folded Sara into her arms and rocked her a bit. They kissed goodbye without a word and let each other go. Sara gave Demetri a hard hug and whispered, "I'll miss you." Then she fled.

During the day at school Sara kept staring out the window. She saw when the first flighty snow came spattering out of the sky and when it turned into a blizzard of frantically whirling flakes. By the time school was out their bus crept along the highway, its windshield wipers fighting to keep a fan of glass clear for the driver, and Sara and Gabe found that the snow lay almost a foot deep as they channeled a path up the driveway. "It's perfect for making a snowman," Gabe said, pressing a ball of it in his hands. "Demi would have loved making a snowman."

"I know." Sara stared at the barn, whose black shape seemed bigger and stronger than ever despite the clinging snow that blotted against it. "The barn's going to seem horribly empty."

"At least Ben's back." Gabe was relieved when he saw

Ben's truck parked inside the barn. "He'll help fill up the space."

"Some of it."

Sara spent a restless evening. She couldn't concentrate on her homework. Blanche skunked her at cribbage. Later, as she walked by the Christmas tree, she accidentally hit a branch, and the needles cascaded from it, leaving a skinny finger she was sure pointed at her in reproof. It had been days since she'd remembered to put water into the crock that held the tree.

Ben noticed the shedding needles. "That tree's mighty dry. Shall I take it down before it sheds all over the floor?"

"It isn't Twelfth Night yet. Richard was planning some kind of thing about taking ornaments off one by one and telling stories and singing songs," Sara reminded him.

"One of his festivals, eh? Well, I won't deprive him of that. We'll have to be extra cheery. I've never seen him as down as he was when he drove Kyra and Demi off this morning."

"Do you think he'll drive back through this snow?" Sara worried.

"It's stopped snowing. Look out the window."

As Sara looked, the full moon seemed to whirl out of the dark clouds as if the wind had hurled it. Then the clouds massed over the moon again, and the sky and the ground were joined in darkness. She watched the headlights of a plow illumine a space where the road lay and puffs of snow fly up away from its blades.

"We ought to be plowing too," Ben said. "Gabe, help me put the blade on my truck and I'll do the driveway. Richard might try to come home tonight."

Sara said, "I'm going to bed. I can hardly keep my eyes open." It wasn't the truth. She didn't want to see her father if he was still as heavy-hearted as Ben reported he'd been when he left.

"That sounds like quite a wind blowing out there," said Harvey. "I'll see that the goats are cozy and the stoves are set for the night. Richard usually does that, but my knees are still good for a trip down below and back."

"Don't bother, Harve. Gabe and I'll take care of everything," Ben told him.

"Then I'll escort Blanche upstairs. Good night, everyone."

Sara saw that Mickey had taken over his usual spot under the pool table. Fonzie leaped onto the chaise vacated by Blanche, trod about in the imprint she'd left in the cushions, and curled into its warmth. Sara hoped Ben would turn out the tree lights. Somehow she needed their twinkle at her back as she left the room.

She was all cuddled into the down comforter Richard had given her for Christmas, with its top pulled over her head and only her nose uncovered, like a seal at its airhole in the ice, when she thought again of the tree. She'd meant to put a bucket of water into its crock after supper and she hadn't done it. She would — first thing in the morning. She listened as Ben chuffed the truck outside and the plow grated back and forth over the gravel. After a while she drowsed off.

Richard's shout awoke Sara. He threw open her door, yanked the bedding off her, and pulled her out onto the floor. "The barn's on fire. Get down to the ramp. Quick!"

Sara gaped at him. She tried to wake up, understand, and start moving, and yet she was only able to go one stage at a time.

"Move!" Richard saw her pants and boots and parka and handed them to her. "Put your legs into your pants. It's cold out. Hurry!"

She managed to pull on the pants, shove her feet into the boots, and haul on her parka, even though her hands were shaking. Richard spread out the comforter he'd pulled off her bed and swept his arm over the top of the bureau, tumbling things down onto it. Sara threw in her clothes that were piled on a chair and made one pass at the top of her shelves, tossing in what she could reach.

"Enough!" Richard twisted the corners of the comforter, making a bundle, handed it to her, and said, "Get going. Down the stairs and out onto the ramp and stay there. Don't come into the barn again. For anything."

"I've got to find Fonzie. He was on Blanche's chaise."

"He was probably the first one out of the barn. Don't argue. Go!"

As he pushed her into the hall, she smelled the smoke. He dashed into the bathroom and wet some washcloths and handed her one. "Put this over your nose and crawl if you have to. I'll see if Harvey needs help."

The door to the Wicketts' room was open, and Richard stepped in. Harvey was urging Blanche to hurry, yet she seemed too stunned to help herself. Richard lifted her to her feet.

Sara fled along the hall, the bundle bumping over her back. She started down the stairs, and the smoke stung in her nostrils. It made her eyes smart, and soon her throat prickled. Each breath drew in more irritating fumes, and she pressed the wet cloth to her nose.

In the common room the smoke was visible, opaque, like a

thick gray wall. She stopped, partly to call "Fonzie!" and partly because she hesitated to step into the smoky gloom. "Don't stop!" Richard yelled from above on the stairs.

She took a deep breath, which made her cough. It hurt all the way down into her chest. Then suddenly she was aware of crackling sounds, like strings of little Chinese firecrackers set off all at once, and she saw something flare into flame, making a towering torch. It was the Christmas tree. She screamed and plunged into the smoke to get away from it. Her eyes streamed so that she could barely see, and through habit alone, she found her way to the next flight of stairs. She held onto the wall until her foot tapped the edge of the first tread and then felt her way down step by step.

Strangely enough, on the ramp level of the barn the smoke wasn't as thick, or else there was more space for it to fill. It was the narrow channel of the stairs that had massed it so thickly. She looked ahead and saw the barn doors were open. Richard's truck was outside, its headlights on to guide the way. She saw, too, twists of flame behind her at the back of the barn and heard their shooting hiss.

"Sara! Come out!" Gabe stood by the truck yelling at her. Mickey was there, barking. Sara tightened her hold on the bundle and ran. It seemed a longer distance than usual to the doors. Each breath rasped in her chest, and the inside of her throat felt as if someone had used a cheese grater on it. Only the frightening glare from the flames now columning up and flaring out behind her kept her running.

Gabe grabbed the bundle and dropped it into the back of the truck. Sara leaned over and threw up. She bent there, gasping and spitting, until she could finally take a deep breath.

"Where are the others?" Gabe's voice cracked with anxiety.

"They were right behind me. Can't you see them yet?"

The lights in the barn had gone off, and there were only the truck headlights beamed into it and the pulsing orange-and-red glow from the flames to see by. The noise of the fire became louder. There was a surflike roar underlying all the snapping and popping of dried-out boards and posts suddenly exploding into flame. Windows cracked from the heat, and streamers of fire pushed through them and crawled up the outside of the barn. Snow that had clotted over the sides and roof in the storm disappeared in a vapor.

"Where are they!" Sara moaned. "Why haven't they come out — "

She and Gabe stared at the drifting smoke and swirling flame, and at last they saw Ben carrying Blanche in his arms and Richard following, with Harvey over his shoulder in a fireman's carry.

"Drop the tailgate," Ben called. Gabe let it down with a clang and helped Ben lay Blanche in the truck. They unbundled the comforter and tucked it around her limp bulk. Her stillness frightened Sara as much as the fire did. "Come sit with Blanche," Ben told her. "You can't do much except hold her hand, but maybe that will help."

Sara climbed into the truck. A frigid wind whipped around her neck as she knelt and picked up Blanche's hand. "You're safe, Blanche. We're all safe." There was no response, even though she gripped Blanche's hand so hard she must have bruised it.

Richard propped Harvey up on the front seat. He was coughing and moaning. "We got Blanche out. As soon as help comes, we'll send her to the hospital."

Richard stood by the truck, and Sara saw him gaze up at

the barn. His cheeks were shiny with tears; she didn't know if they were from the smoke or sorrow at seeing his friends in trouble and his dream disappearing on a burning pyre.

"Did you call the firemen?"

"Ben did. They're coming. God knows they can see where the fire is. It's lighting up the whole sky."

They stood and watched helplessly as flames rocketed out through the cupola, shooting off spangles of sparks.

Richard turned away. "Get into the back of the truck, Gabe. I'll move it so the fire trucks can come closer." He backed the truck off the ramp and parked it on the side of the drive-way, where Ben had left his truck. In a few moments they heard sirens, and the first engine roared in, its equipment rattling and banging as it stopped. Soon three more trucks — two pumpers and a hook-and-ladder — pulled in. The firemen jumped out and began reeling out hoses.

"Looks like that fire is far ahead of us," the chief said. "Everyone out and accounted for?"

Richard looked around. "Everyone *was* out. Where's Ben?"

"He went to let out the goats," Gabe said. "He thinks that back part of the barn may not be so bad yet. Want me to see?"

"No. You stay put. Keep an eye on Harvey. What do you think?" Richard asked the chief. "Can you save any of it?"

The man shook his head. "Got an outside well? Those tanks on the pumpers will run out fast. Or a pond? We could chop through the snow and ice."

"There's no water except what's piped into the house."

"Can't do much then. But we'll give it a try." The chief turned to directing the men. Sara crouched shivering in the truck. She felt as cold now as Blanche's hand.

Gabe looked at Blanche. "How's she doing?"

"I don't know," Sara worried. "Why doesn't an ambulance come! Where did Richard go?"

"To look for Ben. Don't worry — they won't do anything foolish. Hey — you're freezing. Take my parka."

"No. I'll stay down out of the wind. You keep your parka. I wish Richard and Ben would come back!" Sara didn't know whether the strange feeling inside her came from her skin seeming to turn to ice or from terror that her father and Ben would be trapped in the bottom of the barn with the goats.

Dome lights on fire engines, on the chief's car, and on a police car rotated, sending streaks of red-and-blue light lashing out like laser beams. At last another vehicle drove in, and Gabe waved it over. "Over here!" It was the rescue squad.

In seconds Blanche was being eased onto a stretcher and blankets were brought to tuck around her. Gabe rescued Sara's comforter and gave it back to her to wrap up in. The two squad men secured the stretcher in the rescue van. Then one of them helped Harvey, who was having trouble breathing, onto the second stretcher.

As they closed the doors, Gabe asked, "Where are you taking them?"

"To the hospital in Rochester." They slewed into a snowbank as they tried to back down the ramp and lost precious time as they slowly worked their way out of it.

Sara didn't want to sit in the cab, insulated from the sights and sounds. In a ghastly way, there was a hypnotic fascination in staring at the fire. She had to see it clearly. Her only move was to loop the comforter around Gabe too, and they stood huddled together, watching the horror of the blaze. Sara cringed when the sides of the cupola gave way and parts of them slid down the roof. The copper weather vane with its figure of a sturdy cow somersaulted after them, the letters N, S, E, and W whirling madly as it fell, crashing from the roof and disappearing into the snow below.

Richard came up the ramp. "We got the goats out. Ben's tethering them by the kiln. And here's something for you, Sara." He unzipped the top of his parka, and Fonzie stuck his head out.

"Oh, Fonzie! Oh thank you!" Sara tried to hold onto the comforter and Fonzie and couldn't manage both, so she shut him in the cab of the truck. "Where was he?"

"As far away from the smoke as he could get. Down with the goats."

There was a sudden sizzling as a curtain of fire appeared inside the barn at the top of the ramp where the floor was oil-soaked from years of parked vehicles, and then several booms as five-gallon cans of gasoline blew up. The reek of burning oil mingled with the acrid smell of burning wood.

"If there were a kiln in hell it would look like that," Richard murmured.

One of the firemen yelled for them to move the truck farther away. The heat was billowing out as intensely as the flames. Sara realized her face felt seared and only her feet still felt icy. Gabe thrust Mickey into the back of the truck and hopped in after him. Richard backed halfway down to the road. Then they saw cars lining the roadside and people standing by them, watching with great excitement. When part of the roof fell in, there were screams and yells and groans and gasps. Someone even honked his car horn, leaning on it with long blasts.

"That idiot! What does he think this is!" exclaimed Richard. "A fireworks display?"

"Do you think the goats are safe there by the kiln?" Sara asked.

"Ben's still with them I guess. Maybe Gabe and Mickey could watch them. Ben and I ought to be hauling hoses or doing something!" Richard called to Gabe, who leaped into the snow and ran off, with Mickey barking at his heels.

Yet Richard didn't move. He kept gripping the wheel of the truck and staring at the inferno on the hill. "There's not going to be anything left," he groaned. "Ben's furniture. All his tools! My God, he has thousands of dollars' worth of tools! And the tools and things Zeke left. And Harvey's shop. Those miniatures he was going to ship next week!"

"And his money! His desk with all his savings in it — "

"His trip to Tahiti!" There was enough light from the fire filtering into the cab for Sara to see her father's face was black with soot and seared with heat. His expression was clear: It was one of horror and agony.

"Where are we going to live? Blanche and Harvey. And Ben and Zeke. And Gabe! I promised he wouldn't have to go back to his father's house. Oh God! What have I done!" He put his head down on the steering wheel and broke into dry gasps that shook his body. Sara was appalled. Everything was falling to pieces around her. All the bulwarks built up during the summer were crumbling. Kyra had left. The home her father had provided was burning up before her eyes. Something was terribly wrong with Blanche. Harvey's savings were gone. Gabe would be forced to go home. And beside her was her father, devastated by the disaster he felt he had brought down upon them all. She knew only too well how that felt. He needed comforting. He needed to know someone cared. At least she could do that.

Sara leaned her head against his shoulder. "Daddy — " The word came out so naturally that she didn't care that he wanted to be called Richard. "You didn't start the fire. It's not your fault."

"No — but I should have done the things I talked about —got some fire extinguishers, dredged a pond. I should have made Blanche and Harvey move down from that top floor and persuaded Harvey to put his money in the bank. Sara — what about Blanche? I think she fainted. Did she come to?"

"No. I held her hand, and she never moved it. It just felt heavy and cold — " Sara shivered, remembering how the hand had felt. Lifeless. That was how it felt. But she couldn't say it out loud.

"She seemed to collapse when she saw the Christmas tree burst into flame. If Ben hadn't heard me yell and found us and been able to carry Blanche out by himself, I don't think any of us would have made it."

Screams from the onlookers and another honking of car horns made them look up. The great roof timbers, outlined like a silhouetted rib cage where shingles and boards had already burned away, were sagging. The blaze was now so large and brilliant that they couldn't stare at it any more than you could stare at the sun.

"There it goes — that beautiful, noble building!" Richard mourned.

They watched as the rest of the roof caved in. The walls seemed to fold slowly in on top of it, until nothing stood above the ramp level. The firemen had concentrated the water from the tank trucks on the lower part of the structure. Now they were standing about, looking at the steaming, smouldering mess of blackened debris and not able to do anything more about the flames that still fingered the darkness.

"They've run out of water." Richard said. "Will you be all right if I go talk to the chief?"

"Sure. I'll find Gabe." As they left the truck, a van came backing down toward them. On its sides they read the name of a Manchester TV station.

"What are they doing here!" Sara wondered.

"I suppose we're news," Richard said. "The early-morning-disaster headline. Forgotten by tomorrow noon." He slipped in the slush churned up by the vehicles, then carefully made his way toward the fire chief.

Sara found Gabe by the kiln, surrounded by the stamping goats, whose bells let out brittle tatters of sound. "There was a TV crew here taping the fire."

"Richard always said the barn was a landmark. I guess it's news when a landmark burns up. How's Richard doing?"

"Awful! He feels this is his fault and he's let everyone down."

"How can he think the fire's his fault? That's crazy!"

"He certainly thinks the consequences of it are. He cried about it. I didn't know men ever cried."

"I'm going to tell him he's nuts. The goats will be all right now. Come on."

"I tried to tell him," Sara explained as she plunged through the snow after Gabe. "He didn't believe me."

When they found Richard, he was leaning against a fire truck that had run out of water and watching the men, who couldn't do much except pull down rocking timbers and push piles of ashes onto hot spots that flared up. "Well — that's it," he said. "After all the work, all the energy we put into this place. It's all lost."

"Daddy, we're here," Sara reminded him. "You didn't lose us."

Richard pulled Sara close, and he reached out to Gabe too. "Thank God you are here. And safe. I'm even glad now that Kyra and Demi have left. They're safe too."

"Bradford!" the fire chief called. "I need a word with you. How did you discover the fire?"

"I drove in from Boston a little after midnight. The barn was dark, except for a faint light from Harvey's workshop. Then as I parked the truck in the barn, I smelled smoke. I couldn't tell whether it came from above or below, and I didn't see any flames. But the smoke was heavy enough to scare me when I went upstairs. I woke Ben and told him to phone for help. He woke Gabe and I woke the others. It took a while to get everyone out. Before we did, there were flames everywhere."

"And you've accounted for everyone living here? The old man and his wife. The great big guy with the red beard. This young man here and you and your daughter. That's all?"

"Yes."

"Then you didn't know there was someone else in the place?"

"No. We didn't go back into the barn except to get the goats out from their stalls. We didn't check any of the shops, because we were all accounted for. What do you mean — someone else was in the barn!"

"We found a body just now. Right by the door of that shop with the insulated things that look like big ovens —"

"The kilns. In the pottery."

"He looks like a man who lives near you. Named Courbeau. The smoke must have got him."

"My father!" Gabe's words sounded thin, squeezed out of him. "What would my father be doing here?"

# 16

"Would Courbeau have stopped by to help you when he saw the fire?" the chief asked.

Gabe and Richard and Ben looked at each other, wondering.

"I'd like to think so," Richard said slowly. "But I doubt it."

"It's more likely he was here to make trouble," Gabe admitted. "He was probably drunk and came to try again to drag me home."

"Or he might have come to do some damage to Richard's shop, since that's where you found him — or to mine — or to Harvey's," Ben surmised. "He had made some blustery threats to all of us a few weeks ago."

"Has he been hassling you lately, Gabe?" Richard asked.

"No. He didn't speak to me before Christmas, when I took some packages to the kids. Like I told you — he's a brooder. He lets things build up. He's probably been brooding ever since he tried to take me home, and you all stood up for me, about what he'd do to pay us back."

"He wouldn't set a building on fire!" Richard exclaimed. "I can't believe a man would do that, knowing people — especially his own son — were asleep in it."

"It could have been an accident," the fire chief said, aware too late that Gabe was the victim's son. "He might have used matches to see by and dropped them onto something flammable. We can tell more tomorrow. It is a fire of suspicious origin. You should get out of this cold and have some hot food. Is there a place you can go?"

"I should go home and tell my mother about my father," Gabe decided. Sara thought he said it as if he were imposing a sentence on himself. The going home sounded permanent.

Ben heard it too, and put a comforting hand on Gabe's shoulder. "Let me go with you. It's difficult to bring bad news by yourself." He suggested that they also take the goats to the Courbeaus' barn, and the two walked off together.

"Margaret's family could put us up," Sara said. "They're used to having people sleep over. Come on, Daddy."

Richard was too exhausted to think of any other refuge. "I'll go anyplace where there's a bed and a phone. I must find out about Blanche."

As the spectacle of the fire died away, the cars full of on-lookers left. Sara didn't look back when her father drove onto the road. She knew the remains of the barn would be as black against the snow, as sad a ruin, as her future seemed to be. She was on the move again, rootless, her only possessions the jumble of oddments dumped in the back of the truck. The comforter in which she'd brought them out was still wrapped around her, and it bore holes from flying sparks and stains from the snow. She had less than she had arrived with five months before — except then she'd been uncertain about being with her father — how he would accept her; how they would get along together; whether she would like him. Now she knew some of the answers — they could get along together; she wanted to stay with him; she wanted to help him if she could. She did love him, and she hoped he knew he needed her as much as she needed him.

Although it was almost three o'clock in the morning, the lights were on in the Allens' kitchen, and when Sara knocked at the door Margaret and her mother hustled the Bradfords in.

"I'm so glad Roger found you and told you to come," said Mrs. Allen. "I sent him off to get you when I found out the fire was at your place."

"We must have passed him on the road," Richard said. "We came because Sara thought you wouldn't mind putting us up."

"You can stay as long as you need to, my dears. Sara, stand by the stove. Margaret, make her some tea. Mr. Bradford, what would you like? A hot drink? A hot shower?"

"A telephone. I want to call the hospital."

"Let me show you." She took him off.

"How did you know about the fire?" Sara asked. Margaret and her mother both wore bathrobes, but they looked wide-awake.

"My oldest brother, Rick, is a volunteer fireman. Mum heard him leave, and when he didn't come back soon she knew it was a big fire. So she put on the CB, and when she heard where it was she woke up my father and me. Was it scary? I mean, exciting scary or horrible scary?"

"Both." Sara shivered. "Blanche is terribly sick from it or

from the smoke or something. And they found a body and it's Gabe's father."

"Old man Courbeau! Poor Gabe!"

"They think his father was drunk and might have started the fire accidentally. I was scared I'd done it because I'd forgotten to water the Christmas tree. But then I saw the tree when it caught on fire. It went up like an explosion." Sara dropped the soggy comforter and held the cup of tea Margaret gave her in both hands, feeling the heat strengthen her fingers and seep into her wrists.

Richard Bradford came into the kitchen. He pulled out a chair and sat at the table, folding his hands like a small child on the first day of school. He seemed to have trouble controlling his voice.

"Daddy, is it Blanche?"

He nodded.

"Did she die?"

"Yes. Probably while we were taking her out. She had a bad heart and she was frightened. Her heartbeat went haywire, or fibrillated, or whatever they call it. And she died."

Sara went to sit on her father's knees and put her arms around him. "I loved Blanche. She was special."

He held her tightly. "Indeed she was. Blanche of the warm heart and the beatific smile."

"How's Harvey? Does he know?"

"Not yet. He's being treated for smoke inhalation. I'll go see him in the morning."

"I'll go with you."

"Thanks, Sara. My Saradipity." Richard loosened his hold enough so he could look at her. "I have to tell you something right now, because it matters a great deal. I wasn't sure I wanted you to live with me, especially when I was trying to work out my life with Kyra. But I'm glad you came, and I love you very much. Do you think you can stick it out with me no matter what I do next? No matter where I go or how I live?"

"Oh, Daddy! I thought you'd never ask!" Sara didn't care that the words were trite. They said what she meant from her heart.

Mrs. Allen persuaded them to go to bed. "Don't even think about getting up for school, Sara."

"I wish you'd say that to me." Margaret yawned.

Sara, however, could not fall asleep. Her body ached. Nerves still twitched and muscles twanged. If she shut her eyes, images of flames flickered inside her lids. She needed to weep for Blanche, for Harvey, for her father — for all of them who had been happy together for a while in the barn. She didn't want to wake Margaret, who was already asleep in the twin bed a few feet away; but the pain of trying not to cry, the knife-edge in the throat, the stab in the chest, and the twist in the stomach became too much. She put her head under the pillow and let go. She cried until her whole body felt soggy with relief, and she slipped into dreamless sleep.

When she woke the Allens' house was quiet. The clock on the table said ten minutes to ten, and she saw a note beside it: "Use my clothes or anything else you need. Love, Margaret. PS. Have a good day . . . at least as good as you can! Double love, M."

She washed her smoke-tainted hair and showered and put on a borrowed turtleneck and sweater, but she had to wear her own jeans as Margaret's were too big. Mrs. Allen sat in the kitchen rocking chair, holding Fonzie and reading a book. The cat was content with food, company, and rocking, but he al-

lowed Sara to pick him up as Mrs. Allen hurried to the refrigerator.

"Are you hungry?"

"Very." Sara hoped food would quell the feeling she had
of being hollow and breakable.

"That's good." Mrs. Allen produced orange juice and tea,
whisked eggs, and popped toast, with the timed-to-the-second
experience of the mother of six children. "Your father has
gone to see Harvey Wicketts at the hospital."

"I wanted to go with him!"

"He remembered that. But he felt you needed to sleep as
long as you could, and he said if he knew Harvey, he'd be
awake early and asking what had happened to his wife. Anyway, your father will stop to pick you up before he goes to the
barn."

When Richard came into the kitchen a few minutes later,
he carried an armful of things that had been loose in the back
of the truck. "Here's what we rescued. Your lares and penates."

"My what?"

"Lares and penates. Latin for your household gods. In
modern usage, your prized possessions. In this case, your only
possessions."

Sara poked through them. A hairbrush, a bracelet, a small
framed picture of her mother, some mismatched knee socks,
an algebra book, some postcards from Gran, and a small
flocked dog that Bethy-Sue had sent from the county fair —
all the things swept from the top of her bureau; her long
underwear, a velour shirt, and the durable Esmerelda, plucked
from a chair; and from the top of her bookshelves, *Il Coniglio*

*Pierino,* with its familiar pictures of Peter Rabbit, a wood carving of Kiddie that Zeke had given her, and Harvey's Christmas present of an exquisite miniature four-poster bed with the curtains and coverlet made by Blanche, and, with a freshly chipped nose, the Staffordshire cat. "Of all the things I didn't want!" Sara pointed to the cat.

"That thing!" agreed her father. "It looked better in Kyra's painting. Oh God! That painting is gone. I'm sorry. It was a good painting — and it was important to me."

"I'm not sorry. It bothered me because of the cats. I'm sorry that it was the only thing Kyra left with you, though."

"The only *thing,*" her father corrected. "She gave me — she gave all of us — a lot more than a painting."

"I didn't save the photograph she took of you that was on my wall. The one of you sitting in front of a windmill. I loved it."

"If she still has the negative in Crete, she can print you another. Look, I'm supposed to meet the fire chief — at the disaster area."

"I'm ready."

They drove through Martin's Corners, past the school, past the swamp now turned into an arena of snow, past fields that became rolling plains of untrammeled light, past snow fences that cast designs of black upon the white. As they neared the Courbeaus' road, Sara asked, "Can we stop and see Gabe?"

"On the way back. I want to talk with him. And with his mother. He'll have some hard choices to make."

"How do you mean?"

"He's a gifted boy. He can go far, if he's allowed the time he needs for himself. But I think he's loyal too, and now his father's gone he'll want to help his mother and the younger children. It won't be easy for him. But we'll be around. We'll help him all we can."

"You're going to stay here? Near Martin's Corners? Truly?"

"You want that too?" Richard smiled, the first time his eyes had brightened and his face relaxed since the night's turmoil and grief. "I've made up my mind to stay here — even before we see what's left. And to keep the pottery going."

"I do want to stay. I have lots of friends now. And what about Harvey? What's he going to do without Blanche? Without any money?"

"That's the only bright spot. Harvey told me that three days ago he put the money in a bank. He knew Blanche was very ill, and he planned to get her into a hospital. When she was well enough, he was going to take her to Florida to live. When we'd had a chance to catch our breath from Kyra's leaving, he was going to tell us his plans."

"Maybe he'll go to Tahiti by himself. He might want to be far away from where he lived with Blanche."

"He'll miss her no matter where he is. He never wanted to settle for Florida. He only planned it to be easier for her."

"When we fix up a place, could we make room for Harvey?"

"Of course. If he wants to live with us."

The road turned toward the hillside where previously the barn had dominated the view. Sara could not believe that the low patch of rubble lying beyond the ramp was all that was left. It was so small. To its rear was the tree Gabe had liked to swing from onto the deck. The branch supporting the rope had caught fire and was broken off, leaving a tree of unfamiliar shape. The deck had collapsed. Half-burned beams stuck out from the debris in the foundation like shipwrecked timbers, and the sun dazzled on the ice that coated them. Strewn in the yard were various objects pulled from the ruins, looking like flotsam and jetsam on a sea of snow. Among them was the large electric kiln — the one Fonzie had fled to after the punch-bowl catastrophe. Beyond it was the weighted base of a kick wheel and part of its frame.

Richard pulled the truck up beside the fire chief's red car and saw that Ben was sitting in it, talking. He'd left his truck nearby. They got out of the vehicles and stood in a disconsolate circle. Ben asked Sara, "Are you all right?"

Sara nodded. "Have you heard about Blanche?"

"I was almost sure when we laid her down in the truck that she'd gone. You were brave to sit and hold her hand, Sara."

"Mornin'," said the chief. "The fire marshal's man has been and gone, and we've done as much investigating as we can. It looks as if the fire started on the second level, where the woodworking shops were. The timbers were so old, so dry, and there was so much flammable stuff — dried wood, gas cans —"

"A dry Christmas tree," Sara admitted.

"And with that wind last night and not enough water — and to say, there was no way of stopping it. There'll be a gap in the landscape without it, all right. Built about eighteen fifty, I believe."

"Any idea how it started?"

"Anybody a smoker?"

"No cigarettes."

"I smoked a pipe after supper," said Ben. "But I never smoked in the shop."

"That fellow whose body we found — Courbeau there — had a plastic bag full of match folders on him. My guess is, since he was obviously where he didn't belong, that he caused it. He could have been using matches to see by instead of a flashlight. He could have dropped a match — either accidentally or on purpose. We'll never know. You can believe what you want. Now, you should get a wrecker in here, haul that rubble out, or get a bulldozer to push it over and fill in the foundation. You don't want kids playing in that wreckage."

"I'll see to it," Richard promised. After the chief left he said, "Haul it all out or push it all in! What a way to talk about your home."

"We should haul it out," Ben said. "Then we can see what shape the foundation's in." He spoke so positively, but then he stopped, looking embarrassed. "I mean, if you want to think about rebuilding on it. After this, you may want to go off — take up traveling again."

"Not with Sara in school and her friends here. Not with Gabe to give a hand to. Not with Harvey needing a place. Not with a good business like Earthforms to continue. And you, Ben, what about you?"

"Look at the angle of that foundation. Perfect for a solar construction. I got to thinking about it last night. Look — " He began to draw in a clear patch of snow. Sara heard the excitement in the men's voices. Shop and dwelling units in a row on the old foundation. Active solar systems for heat and hot water. Maybe a windmill for electricity. "And Zeke will want to be in on it too." Ben was sure.

"It could be more livable than the barn," Richard agreed. "More comfortable housing. Better-organized shop space. Each of us could have a unit that would combine shop and living space. More private, but still a community. I like your idea. Thanks for standing by, Ben, and for wanting to put things back together again. You're a real friend."

"Purely selfish on my part," said Ben. "I know a good thing when I'm living in it. As to Gabe and his mother, I think they'll be better off without the old man around. Mrs. Courbeau looks about ready to pop child number nine, but she was up this morning, straightening up that kitchen and washing things as if there was finally some point in doing it again."

"How about Gabe?"

"He can make it. He's got both guts and feelings. He might need a corner of your new pottery for an escape hatch now and then."

"He'll have it," Richard promised. "We'll be along to see him in a little while."

Ben drove off. Sara followed Richard around the debris-strewn yard.

"I can really see it," Richard said, overlooking the rubble thoughtfully. "Would you like to be a pioneer of the solar age, Sara?"

"That would be fantastic!" She was relieved to see that he was glad of Ben's suggestions and cooperation, and to feel — suddenly to be sure — that she could trust him to make the best of the situation.

She could trust him! She gave him an enthusiastic hug. His cap fell off, and he stood there with his hair wisped up in the wind, his face unshaven, his tired eyes red-rimmed, and his clothes stinking with smoke. She thought there wasn't a twinkle left in him, and then she saw it — the glint in his eye. She could sense his natural enthusiasm rising up and his energy rekindling, and she was glad to see it.

For a moment she didn't feel the cold snapping of the wind at her face. She didn't feel the desolation of the ice-glittered ruin beyond them.

She picked up his hat and jammed it onto his head. "What do we do first?"

"That's my girl!" Richard gave her a joyful smile. "That's my Saradipity."

"Remember when you told me about wanting to name me Serendipity? You said it was because it meant something happy that you discover by accident?"

"I do remember. You rather took umbrage."

"I took *what?* Never mind that word now. What I want to say is — that if we were playing Dictionary and if Saradipity was the word to define, I've thought of a definition for it. Can you guess?"

"You look so pleased about it, you'd better tell me. Don't keep me in suspense."

"It's so obvious. Saradipity means something happy that you discover you had all the time."

"Very well said, Sara. And now we've been through so much together, here's my discovery. I'm proud to be your father."